★

"What's this?"

"Photos taken at the scene."

She sat down beside him and studied the pictures of the victims for several minutes.

One photo showed a man sprawled, faceup, on the floor. She'd seen enough TV shots of Senator Jason Ritchie to recognize him instantly. Apparently he'd been shot in the right side of his neck. Though his coat and shirt were bloodied, she was surprised there wasn't more blood. He must have died soon after he was shot, she decided. On the floor beside the body she noticed an open briefcase.

In the other photo a woman was slumped on a couch, her long, slender legs dangling awkwardly from her miniskirt, as if she'd fallen backward, or been pushed. Her hair was in disarray. She looked as if she'd struggled to defend herself against the assailant.

"Nadine Berkman of the *National Informer*," Liz murmured. "I wonder how that scandal sheet will treat one of its own?"

★

Previously published Worldwide Mystery title by
DOROTHY P. O'NEILL

DOUBLE DECEPTION

FATAL
PURCHASE

Dorothy P. O'Neill

WORLDWIDE®

TORONTO • NEW YORK • LONDON
AMSTERDAM • PARIS • SYDNEY • HAMBURG
STOCKHOLM • ATHENS • TOKYO • MILAN
MADRID • WARSAW • BUDAPEST • AUCKLAND

Recycling programs
for this product may
not exist in your area.

FATAL PURCHASE

A Worldwide Mystery/April 2011

First published by Avalon Books

ISBN-13: 978-0-373-26749-1

Printed in U.S.A.

Acknowledgments

With thanks to
Alison Bouwmeester, U.S. Department of State
Paul Edward Cox, Special Agent, FBI
Robert Pentz Barlow, M.D.

PROLOGUE

BEHIND A COUNTER in the lingerie department of Sohms Fifth Avenue, Angie Diaz suppressed a yawn and looked at her watch. It had been a slow, boring morning so far, and she still had more than an hour to go till her lunch break. Almost wistfully, she recalled the hectic Christmas shopping season a few months ago.

"I am ready to fall asleep over here," she called across the aisle to Shondra at the bra-and-panties counter. Shondra had been fairly busy this morning, but nobody was buying expensive nightgowns or negligees.

"Cheer up," Shondra called back. "A man just got off the elevator."

Good, Angie thought. When men ventured into the lingerie department they usually bought expensive birthday or anniversary gifts. Hastily, she arranged a few of the priciest nightgowns on the countertop. Many male customers were uncomfortable buying lingerie and pounced on the first item they saw.

"Good morning," she said to the tall gentleman approaching her counter. He was carrying a briefcase. He looked like a wealthy businessman, she thought.

It took her a few seconds to realize who he was. *Massachusetts Senator Jason Ritchie.* There was no mistaking his distinguished bearing and the silvery hair crowning his handsome face. His frequent television appearances had made him as recognizable as any Hollywood star.

Her smile faded into a frown. If it hadn't been for Senator Ritchie's recent restrictive immigration bill, her mother and brother would be with her, now, instead of living in the wretched poverty of their Colombian village. Rules of the new legislation did not consider the fact that she intended to become an American citizen as soon as she was eligible and the Bureau of Immigration had ignored her plea that *Mamacita* was frail and sick and unable to continue her job cleaning the *padre*'s house, and *Hermano* forced to drop out of the church school and take whatever menial jobs he could get. She sent them as much money as she could and felt guilty she could not send more.

She had come to the United States more than four years ago on a visa as a child's nanny. Although she could speak a little English, she enrolled in night school and studied every chance she got until she knew how to read, write and speak the language correctly. After that, she spent most of her spare time in the public library, reading everything she thought might improve her language skills. Now she spoke fluent, almost flawless English.

It had not been easy, but she had worked hard and stuck to her goals of getting a job with a future, saving what money she could and bringing Mama and Hermano to the States. Now, here she was, soon to be promoted to assistant buyer, and assured by the Director of Personnel that she had a bright future at Sohms. She was able to send for them now, but…anger boiled inside of her. Her resentment of Senator Jason Ritchie was close to hatred.

The senator's resonant voice penetrated her thoughts. "How are you this fine day, young lady?"

As if he cared, Angie thought. She managed a smile. "I am fine, thank you, sir." She could tell he was accustomed to being recognized. She would not give him the satisfaction of knowing she realized who he was.

It bothered her, knowing this anti-Hispanic senator was running for his political party's presidential nomination. From what she had heard, he did not have a chance. His anti-Latino stand would work against him. But she knew his stand against government waste of money—and his reputation as a man of the highest moral character—had made him popular with many Americans. Some religious people especially liked the way he included quotations from the Bible in his political speeches. Others ridiculed him for injecting morality into his speeches, saying he sounded more like a preacher than a politician. They called him names like "Senator Spotless" and "The Saintly Senator." Some political cartoonists depicted him with a halo around his head.

Political polls showed him trailing every other candidate for the nomination. But this did not mean it would not happen. What if he did win the nomination and went on to be elected president? The thought chilled her. With an anti-Latino in the White House, her chances of bringing her family to the United States might be slimmer than ever.

She forced a smile. "How may I help you, sir?" she asked.

"I'd like to look at some nightgowns," he replied. "Black silk with lace."

None of the nightgowns she'd displayed on the counter were black. Nodding, she put them aside. "Certainly, sir. What size? They run from small to extra large."

"Extra large," he said, without hesitation.

Most men were not so sure about size, Angie thought, while she brought out the black nightgowns. How many times had she been appraised and asked what size she wore? They would compare her with their wives or mothers before deciding.

"These are all pure silk and the lace is handmade," she told him, arranging four black nightgowns on the counter. Except for one, she had deliberately brought out modestly styled gowns. She had seen the Saintly Senator's wife on television. Mrs. Ritchie was a prim-looking little woman who appeared as if she'd never wear anything low-cut or revealing in or out of bed.

The senator eyed the garments. He touched the lace bodice of the only nightgown Angie believed his wife would not wear and ran his hand slowly over its silken folds.

"Very nice," he said. "This one will do."

Angie took his credit card and recorded the sale. No doubt he had noticed she did not recognize him and now he was probably waiting for her to say something when she saw his name on the card.

"Oh, you are Senator Jason Ritchie! I thought I knew you but I was not sure. May I have your autograph?"

When she said nothing, she sensed his annoyance at not being recognized. He considered himself a celebrity, she decided. He must be very arrogant to believe he could be nominated for President of the United States.

"I'd like to have this delivered to my hotel today," he said. "I have to attend a luncheon right after I leave here and then a meeting. I won't get back to the hotel till after six. I don't want to carry a parcel around with me all day."

"We generally do not deliver until the day after purchase," Angie said, "but we make exceptions if it is a special gift. Shall I have the nightgown gift wrapped? That way there will be no problem having it delivered to your hotel today."

He gave a brusque nod. "All right, go ahead and have it gift wrapped."

"What hotel are you staying at, Mr. Ritchie?"

"The Waldorf." His blunt reply told her she had annoyed him all the more by this further indication that she had not recognized him—saying *Mr.* instead of *Senator.*

She could not resist one more jab. "If you will excuse me for a few minutes, Mr. Ritchie, I will make arrangements for the gift wrapping and find out what time the delivery can be made."

"It's *Senator* Ritchie," he replied.

"Senator Ritchie," she said, forcing a smile. Maybe he would take the smile to mean she had recognized him at last. This was all she intended to do. She would not fawn over this arrogant anti-Latino.

She made the arrangements and returned to the counter.

"Your package will be delivered by six o'clock

this evening," she said. "Will that be satisfactory, Senator?"

He nodded. "That's fine. It can be left at the lobby desk and I'll pick it up when I get there." Now that he believed he had been recognized, he put on the warm smile so familiar to TV viewers. "Thanks for suggesting the gift wrapping. It's important to me to have it this evening."

Evidently he wanted his prim little wife to wear black silk lace during their night at the Waldorf Astoria, Angie thought, as she handed him his credit card receipt.

"Thanks again and God bless you," he said.

Watching him walk towards the elevators, Angie understood why many Americans liked him. Except for the few minutes when he thought she had not recognized him, he had seemed quite friendly. Besides being very handsome and having a reputation as a man of the highest moral standards, he had that rare *encanto* Americans called charisma. It was hard to believe he was prejudiced against Latinos. He must have picked up on her accent and her dark hair and eyes, but she had not noticed the slightest negative attitude. Maybe he thought she was from Spain. The Castillian Spanish people were acceptable to him and others like him. It was only the poor *Sudo-Americanos* they wanted to keep out of the country.

Again, her anger and resentment flared. She took a deep breath to calm herself. Getting angry would not help her bring Mama and Hermano here. Like the woman at the Bureau of Immigration told her, she must be patient. Under the terms of the new regulations, everything took longer.

She tried to drive her frustration away by picturing the senator presenting the gift wrapped nightgown to his wife. How would she react when she saw the low cut, revealing lace bodice? Then, suddenly, it struck her. The senator's wife was *little!* In television shots of her with her husband, she barely came up to his shoulder. Also, she did not look as if she weighed much more than one hundred pounds. There was no way this very small woman would wear an extra large size.

Now she recalled reading an item in this morning's newspaper that Senator Ritchie was attending a political function in New York today, and that Mrs. Ritchie had remained in Washington. She remembered the nightgown's low cut, lace bodice and the way he had fondled it, and knew there could be only one explanation. The Saintly Senator had purchased it for some other woman, and the woman was not his mother or sister.

As if her mind were a computer, an idea clicked in and then a scheme flashed on. This was her chance to get even with Senator Ritchie. She could ruin his reputation as a man of high moral standards and end whatever chance he had for getting the presidential nomination. Besides being exposed as a faithless husband, he would be branded a hypocrite.

She would go to one of the newspapers with her story. To back it up she had the sales receipt with today's date and a description of the merchandise sold. *Black silk nightgown XL.* It was fortunate she had developed the habit of including the size on her receipts to keep track of the inventory. And below the incriminating XL was the signature of the man responsible for keeping her and her loved ones apart.

He would not be known as the Saintly Senator much longer, she thought. She brushed away her misgivings. There was no need to feel guilt and tell herself that his chances of getting the nomination were slim and by doing this she would only cause trouble in his marriage.

What did that matter? She would be causing him pain, just as he had caused pain for her and her family. Suddenly she felt giddy with excitement.

She knew exactly where she would go. Not to any of New York's three big newspapers. She knew where her story would get immediate attention and she would be paid for it, too. On her lunch break she would go to the paper that printed scandal. She would take her information to the *National Informer*.

AT HER DESK IN THE OFFICES of the *National Informer,* Nadine Berkman scrutinized the Sohms sales receipt. She pushed her dark rimmed glasses back over her dyed auburn bangs and looked at Angie with a grin.

"This will make a great story," she said. "We'd just about given up hoping someone would come in with a little dirt on Senator Spotless. I know you have to take this receipt back to the store, so let me make a copy of it, then I'll pay you for the information."

Angie watched her step away from her desk and run the receipt twice through a copy machine. This was even easier than she'd expected.

"I'm prepared to pay you two hundred dollars," Nadine said, returning to her desk and giving Angie back the original receipt. "If that's okay with you, just sign this release and I'll write you a check."

Two hundred dollars! Angie felt a surge of joy. She had not expected so much. It would go a long way towards making life better for Mama and Hermano.

"Well, how about it?" Nadine asked. "Is it a deal?"

"Yes, of course." Angie could not believe how easy it had been. She had just walked in and approached the first desk with someone sitting at it. This Nadine Berkman did not even have to consult with anyone or ask anyone's opinion. She must have an important job on the paper.

Nadine handed her the check. She had signed it herself, Angie noticed. She did not need anyone else's signature. Yes, she was important.

"This looks like a personal check, but it's on one of the paper's accounts," Nadine explained. "The bank's just down the block. You can get this cashed on your way back to the store."

"When will the story be in the paper?" Angie asked.

"Not right away. We'll probably wait till just before the next State Primary."

The story would be damaging whenever it broke, Angie thought. Feeling lighthearted, she left the newspaper offices and went to the bank, where the sight and feel of two hundred dollars in bills added to her euphoria. Mama and Hermano would eat well for the next few months, and maybe after that she would get some good news from Immigration.

On her way back to Sohms, she wondered if she should tell Juan what she had done. Juan Vega was a Puerto Rican. He worked as a clerk for Garcia y Morales, a firm which handled legal cases for Hispanics. They had met in the library a few months ago and become friends. He was her only friend in New York. She had been drawn to him because, like her, he believed Latinos entering this country should learn English and become assimilated into the American mainstream—not cling to the Spanish language and live in barrios and associate only with other Latinos.

Lately, her feelings for Juan had grown beyond friendship, and she sensed he, too, felt this. They were falling in love, she thought, with a dreamy smile.

Juan called himself a Nationalist and did a lot of talking about Puerto Rican independence. And because Senator Ritchie had taken a strong stand against independence for Puerto Rico, Juan disliked him as much as she did. Juan would get a laugh out of knowing the senator was nothing but a hypocrite. He would applaud her for going to the scandal newspaper with the nightgown story.

She was meeting him after work for coffee this evening. Yes, she would tell him everything.

SMILING, NADINE LEANED BACK in her chair and stared at the two copies she'd made of the Sohms sales receipt. The instant she'd seen the signature, a plan had started unfolding in her mind. What a stroke of good luck that her boss was out when this Angelita Diaz appeared in the office. The two hundred out of her own pocket was chicken feed compared to what she could get from Senator Spotless.

The hush money would be her ticket out of this sleazy job and an escape from her stormy relationship with

Kurt. She'd get out of town and never have to put up with his jealous rages again.

When she'd questioned Angelita, she'd found out the senator was staying at the Waldorf Astoria and the nightgown would be delivered there around six this evening. The senator wouldn't get there till after six. She'd leave the office in plenty of time to wait in the lobby near the desk, till she saw the senator come in. She'd recognize him instantly from TV appearances. She'd watch him pick up his parcel and then she'd approach him as he walked to the elevator. She'd tell him she wanted to interview him for an article she was writing for her newspaper; she'd say the subject was America's declining morality. He'd go for that.

Her smile broadened. If the senator was as big a hypocrite as it seemed, she might not even have to hand him the line about an interview. He might jump at a chance to get her into his hotel room, even if she wasn't voluptuous enough to wear a size extra large.

But, would there be time for her to make her pitch, collect what cash she could as a first installment and get out of there before Ms. Extra Large arrived for the rendezvous?

Yes, she decided. Angelita had been so excited about getting two hundred dollars for her story, she'd answered every question without hesitation. She'd said the senator was going to be out all afternoon at a luncheon and then a meeting.

He'd want to shower and shave before the recipient of the black silk nightgown got there, Nadine decided. Most likely he didn't expect her for an hour or more. Anyway, the shakedown wouldn't take long. One look at that sales receipt and Senator Spotless would give little Nadine anything she wanted for as long as she wanted it.

The gift that would keep on giving. Her smile escalated into a laugh.

ONE

LIZ ROONEY WATCHED the evening news with growing fascination. Earlier reports of a double murder at the prestigious Waldorf Astoria Hotel had been sketchy, saying only that a man judged to be in his mid-fifties had been found shot to death in his suite, along with a woman in her late-twenties or early-thirties.

Until this moment, no names had been given. Now the identity of the slain couple burst off the screen via a network newscaster.

"Just in—an update of the double murder at the Waldorf Astoria Hotel. The victims have been identified as United States Senator Jason Ritchie of Massachusetts and Nadine Berkman, a reporter on the staff of the *National Informer.*"

Liz shook her head in disbelief. The Saintly Senator dead in a hotel room with a female tabloid reporter half his age? Impossible, she thought. It didn't add up.

On second thought, she'd followed enough murder cases to know nothing was impossible. She'd been hooked on homicides since she was a kid. As the daughter of a NYPD homicide detective, she got all the encouragement she needed. Pop often told her she'd make a good detective herself.

A recent photo of the female murder victim flashed onto the screen. An attractive young woman, Liz thought, though somewhat hard-looking. That long mass of bright red hair had to be straight out of a bottle. She fingered a lock of her own hair. A natural redhead could spot a phony every time.

The news ended. She switched off the TV and glanced at her watch. Eichle would be here soon. She was still surprised that Detective George Eichle had phoned earlier and said he wanted to come over and discuss the Waldorf murders with her. This was a big switch from his former hostility, dating back to the first time he encountered her at a murder scene with her boss, Medical Examiner Dan Switzer. Eichle had mellowed since then, but she couldn't forget how he'd snapped at her—as if he hadn't known her since the days when Pop brought his hooked-on-homicides teenager into the station house, and as if he wasn't aware that Dan and Pop were close friends and Dan encouraged her passion for following murder cases, too.

"What are you doing here, Rooney?" Eichle had snarled.

"I'm with the medical examiner, Eichle," she'd retorted.

They'd been calling each other by their last names ever since. As long as that continued, she thought there'd always be a trace of animosity.

Eichle knew that Dan had given her a job in his office after college. In forensic records. Nothing to do with the physical part of the medical examiner's office. This Eichle had found out from Pop. Before Pop retired from the force and he and Mom moved to Florida, he and Eichle worked together and struck up a friendship.

"George Eichle's the brightest young cop I've known in a long time," Pop used to say.

But it wasn't his friendship with Pop that softened Eichle's hostility towards her. His attitude had mellowed after she came up with a clue in a recent homicide and let him in on it.

However, she sensed he still resented her presence at crime scenes. When he phoned earlier and said he wanted to come over that night, she was sure he just wanted to gloat because he knew Dan was on vacation and she hadn't been able to go to the crime scene this time.

Her thoughts returned to Senator Jason Ritchie. She found it hard to believe someone would want to kill him. Not that she was a fan of the evangelical senator. Though she admired his reputation for honesty and integrity, she disliked the bill he'd sponsored, severely limiting Latin-American immigration. She'd been brought up to believe all worthy immigrants should have a chance to come here. It was surprising the bill was passed in a political climate favorable to Hispanics. Pop said the senator had managed to get it through as part of a measure against drug smuggling.

The doorbell rang. She made sure she saw Eichle's shock of sandy hair and his hazel eyes through the peephole before opening the door.

He'd barely stepped inside before he glanced at her TV, saying, "If you've been watching the news, I guess you heard the male victim of the Waldorf shootings is Senator Jason Ritchie."

She nodded. "Yes, I heard. I can't believe it."

"Believe it," he replied. She was sure he meant he'd

seen the body and she hadn't. Was he rubbing it in because she hadn't been at the crime scene this time?

"You told me you weren't coming over here to gloat," she said.

He flashed a grin, saying, "Don't get your redheaded temper up." He took an envelope out of his pocket and handed it to her. "Here—have a look."

"What's this?"

"Photos taken at the scene. I thought they might make up for not being able to get there."

"Thanks." She cast him a questioning glance as she motioned for him to sit down on the sofa. "I can't get used to you being so nice."

"I thought we got past that," he said. "Go ahead and look at the photos."

She sat down beside him and studied the pictures of the victims for several minutes.

One photo showed a man sprawled, face-up, on the floor. She'd seen enough TV shots of Senator Jason Ritchie to recognize him instantly. Apparently he'd been shot in the right side of his neck. Though his coat and shirt were bloodied, she was surprised there wasn't more blood. He must have died soon after he was shot, she decided. On the floor beside the body she noticed an open briefcase.

In the other photo a woman was slumped on a couch, her long, slender legs dangling awkwardly from her mini skirt, as if she'd fallen backwards, or been pushed. Her hair was in disarray. She looked as if she'd struggled to defend herself against the assailant. Bloodstains indicated she'd been shot in the chest, but Liz noticed she'd bled even less than the senator. Death must have been instantaneous.

"Nadine Berkman of the *National Informer*," Liz murmured. "I wonder how that scandal sheet will treat one of its own?"

The absence of anything in the scene to suggest a clandestine rendezvous seemed strange to her. Though the table next to the couch was clearly visible, she saw none of the clichéd trappings of a tryst, such as a champagne bottle in a bucket of ice, two stemmed glasses, an elaborate arrangement of flowers. But something caught her eye. The camera hadn't included it totally, but on the table next to the couch she saw part of what was unmistakably a large, flat box tied up with fancy ribbon.

"Looks like it was somebody's birthday," she said. "Had the box been opened when you got to the scene?"

"No," Eichle replied. "It looked like it had just come from the store."

"I guess you opened the box to see what was in it, then tied it up again."

"Good guess."

"So, what was in it?"

"A fancy black silk nightgown."

"It doesn't figure. The bodies were discovered by the maid this morning, weren't they? Rather late in the morning, according to the news broadcast I heard."

He smiled. "Your father always said you'd make a good detective, Rooney. You're thinking the box should have been opened last night and the nightgown taken out."

"So why wasn't it?" The instant she asked the question, the answer came to her. The senator and his companion were murdered last night, before he had a chance to present her with the nightgown.

"Well, have you figured it out?" he asked.

"I think so. They probably hadn't been in the room very long before it happened. Someone could have gained access to the room by pretending to be a member of the hotel staff—like a maintenance man checking on the plumbing or heating. It could have been an attempted robbery that got out of hand."

Eichle nodded. "The coroner estimated the deaths occurred some time during the early evening. I agree the killer could have gotten into the room the way you suggested, but the robbery motive doesn't wash. Their wallets hadn't been taken."

Liz glanced at the photos again. From her experience at crime scenes where shooting was involved, it looked as if the Waldorf victims had been shot at close range.

"The murderer was close to them when the shots were fired," she said.

"Right. The coroner believes the woman died almost immediately, but the senator stayed alive for a few minutes. You probably noticed the briefcase near the senator's body. After the photo was taken, we found a cell phone in there. We figure he tried to get it to call for help."

"Didn't anyone report hearing the shots?"

"No, but that's understandable. The suite's located

at the end of a corridor, and the adjacent suites were unoccupied."

Was this a straight answer or could the gun have been equipped with a silencer? She sensed he was withholding information about the gun.

He must have guessed her thoughts. "You know I can't give you confidential police information, but if you ask questions I can answer, I will," he said.

He meant he'd give her the same information she'd hear on tomorrow's TV news or in the newspaper, she thought. But she knew she shouldn't complain. He'd shown her the crime scene photos and that was next best to being there.

"Have the bullets been sent to the police lab to find out what kind of gun was used?" she asked.

Eichle shook his head. "No need for that. The killer left the gun at the scene. We found it near the senator's body."

"The gun was left behind?" Liz asked, in surprise. "Why would any killer do that?"

"Panic," he said. "It happens."

"Like when?"

"When someone doesn't intend to pull the trigger, but only brings out the gun to scare someone else, and when the gun goes off she can't think of anything except getting out of there."

"*She?* That sounds as if you think women are more likely to panic than men."

"In my experience, they are."

"So you think the killer is a woman?"

"I didn't say that."

But that's what he was thinking, she decided. Was it possible he suspected the senator's wife? Maybe Mrs. Ritchie found out her husband had been playing around. Maybe she'd found out about the rendezvous at the Waldorf. Maybe she'd decided to confront him. Maybe she'd flown to New York soon after he left and posted herself in the lobby to spy on him after he got there. She saw her husband pick up a gift wrapped box at the desk, then meet a young woman in the lobby. She watched them go up on the elevator together. She followed them and got into the suite by pretending to be a maid.

As Eichle said, she didn't intend to use the gun. She only wanted to scare the daylights out of them. But if both the senator and the woman tried to get the gun away from her, it could have gone off in the struggle and killed both of them. Then Mrs. Ritchie panicked and fled without the gun.

"Any fingerprints on the gun?" she asked.

"Too smudged to lift. Whose prints did you think would be there?"

"Whose prints did *you* think you'd find?"

"I'm waiting to see who registered the gun before I think about that," he replied.

Again she sensed he was holding back information about the gun. He hadn't even told her what kind it was. But, whether he admitted it or not, she was sure he suspected the killer was a woman, and the senator's wife could be that woman.

"Do you think Mrs. Ritchie did it?" she asked.

"I guess there's no harm in telling you. It's my personal opinion that Mrs. Ritchie could be a suspect."

"Because she had a motive?"

"The oldest motive in the history of crime. Sure, she was supposed to stay in Washington while the senator went to New York, but she could have flown up here after he left."

Liz liked knowing her deductions were the same as a seasoned detective's. "So, after you check the airlines and the gun registration, you'll know if Mrs. Ritchie might be the guilty one," she said.

"Let's just say we'll know if she's a suspect," he replied.

"I guess she's come to Manhattan by now. Do you know where she's staying?"

"She got here late this afternoon. She's with friends. I'm going to interview her tomorrow morning."

"Will you let me know what you find out?"

"I can't make any promises."

"Well, thanks for telling me what you could and especially for letting me see the photos."

"I haven't forgotten you helped crack the last case."

"Maybe I can help crack this one, too. I'll let you know what I come up with."

"Good citizen," he said, with a grin. "Any questions before I go?"

"Just one. Why weren't the bodies found sooner? The senator must have brought one of his aides to Manhattan with him. Have you questioned the aide?"

"Senator Ritchie didn't bring anyone with him." Eichle replied. "He seldom took aides along on brief trips. He considered it a waste of taxpayers' money."

Saving taxpayers' money was the last thing on the

senator's mind when he made this trip to New York, Liz thought.

Apparently Eichle had told her all he was going to, for now.

"Before you leave, how about coffee?" she asked.

"Great, thanks."

"I could throw in a doughnut if you'd like."

"I'd like," he said.

AFTER SHE GOT INTO BED that night, she reviewed the evening's talk. It pleased her that she and Eichle were on the same page. But it didn't take much sleuthing talent this time to figure things out, she told herself. If the killer was indeed a woman, then Mrs. Ritchie was the logical one.

Or was she?

Suddenly, she recalled the photo of the woman victim as clearly as if she were looking at it again. Had Eichle assumed, as she had, that the nightgown was bought for her? Images of the woman and the nightgown whirled in her head. She switched on her lamp and looked up Eichle's number in the phone book.

"Eichle? It's me, Rooney."

"Rooney—what's up?"

"I was thinking about the nightgown."

"Yeah? What about it?"

"Did you notice what size it was?"

"Sure—extra large."

"That means it wasn't bought for the woman who was killed. She was very slender. She would have worn a small size." Her thoughts were coming so fast now; she could scarcely put them into words. "Maybe it wasn't Mrs. Ritchie who came into the suite last night. Maybe the woman the nightgown was intended for came in, and when she saw the senator with that reporter she didn't stop to think it might have been an innocent meeting. She lost her cool and…" She paused for breath.

"Pretty good reasoning, Rooney," Eichle said.

He didn't sound at all surprised. It was as if he'd known about the discrepancy in sizes all along. She felt foolish. "Sorry I bothered you," she said. "I didn't know for sure if you'd noticed the woman victim was small."

"I get paid to notice those things," he replied. "But, like I said, it was pretty good thinking. I hope you'll keep on telling me your ideas."

Then, as if he sensed she felt foolish and he wanted to ease her feelings, he added, "I'll phone you at work tomorrow, Rooney, and let you know if there's anything else I can discuss with you."

She was about to thank him when he added, "But don't expect to hear from me till afternoon. I'll be tied up at the *National Informer* most of the morning."

Now he was patronizing her, she thought. She didn't like this much better than his former disapproving attitude. When a sudden idea popped into her mind, she went with it.

"Did you notice if there was a store name on the nightgown box?" she asked.

"Sure—Sohms Fifth Avenue," he replied. "Why?"

"Just curious," she said.

She smiled as she hung up the phone. She wasn't going to wait most of tomorrow while he decided whether or not to tell her more about the case. Tomorrow, on her lunch break, she'd drop into the lingerie department of Sohms and do a little investigating of her own.

TWO

Liz got off the elevator in Sohms and headed for the lingerie department. With a little luck, she might encounter the sales clerk who'd waited on Senator Ritchie. She wanted to find out if he'd been accompanied by a woman. If it turned out he'd had a woman companion with him she wanted to ask some questions.

She already knew the woman who was with the senator when they were shot was not the one for whom the nightgown was purchased. If she could get a description of the woman who was in Sohms with the senator that day, she'd have something to tell Eichle.

"May I show you something, miss?" asked a sales clerk behind the counter.

As a means to hang around the lingerie department awhile without arousing suspicion, Liz had already decided to buy Mom something for her upcoming birthday. She glanced at a display above the showcase. "Yes," she replied. "Those slips up there are lovely but I don't see peach color. Do you have it in peach?"

"I'm sorry, miss—that style only comes in those colors, but we have others in peach. Would you like to see them?" Liz noticed she spoke with a slight Hispanic accent.

"Yes, thank you," Liz replied, "in a medium."

The sales clerk was a pretty young woman, probably

Mexican or South American, judging from her rich Spanish accent and her dark hair and eyes. Had she been here when the senator made his fatal purchase yesterday? With the murder story all over the news, surely she'd remember waiting on him and recall if there was a woman with him.

As a way to start talking about the Waldorf murders, Liz had brought this morning's *New York Times* with her. While the clerk went to get the peach color slips, she put the newspaper on the counter, folded to show the article about the murders. Too bad the *Daily News* hadn't hit the newsstands yet. Its sensational, tabloid style would be much more conducive to striking up a conversation about the case. If the *News* had found out about the nightgown they'd have featured it on the front page. It wasn't even mentioned in the *Times*.

The clerk returned and displayed the slips on the countertop, saying, "Here they are, miss…" She looked startled and disturbed when she saw the newspaper.

"Terrible about that senator and the young woman, wasn't it?" Liz said.

"Yes, terrible…" The clerk's voice quivered. She seemed distraught all of a sudden, Liz thought. A thought flashed into her mind. *Bingo!* This must be the sales clerk who'd sold the black nightgown to the senator.

"I always heard he was a fine man, devoted to his wife. I just can't believe he was in his hotel room with another woman," Liz said.

She pretended to examine the slips, while keeping a furtive eye on the sales clerk. "They're all lovely. I can't quite make up my mind which one," she said.

The clerk glanced at the headline in the newspaper again, and again Liz noticed she seemed unduly disturbed. Strange, Liz thought. The senator was known to be anti-Latino. The sales clerk was most certainly from a country affected by his harsh immigration legislation. Surely she didn't feel too much grief over his death.

"I can see you're upset by Senator Ritchie's murder," she said. "So am I. I've always admired him for his character, even if I often disagreed with his political views." She paused to allow the sales clerk to reply.

The clerk seemed to hesitate before asking, "Have you decided which slip you want?"

Liz got the feeling she'd been about to make an entirely different response, most likely something in connection with the senator. "Not yet," she replied. She pretended to concentrate on the slips again. Time to bring out the big guns, she thought. Deliberately, she let her gaze wander from the slips to the newspaper. "I can't understand how Senator Ritchie could be so hardhearted towards Latino immigrants," she said.

That did it. Liz was startled by the almost explosive reply.

"Hardhearted. Yes, if he had a heart at all. I know I should not speak ill of the dead, but I must tell you how cruel this man was. His new immigration law has kept my mother and brother out of this country, even though my mother is not well and they are living in poverty and even though I am able to provide for them if they are allowed to come here. I am only one of many trying to bring relatives here, but it is always the same story. We are told under the new law it takes more time. My mother is without medical care. I am afraid she might die before I see her and my brother again."

Shocked, Liz could not keep from clasping the distressed young woman's hand. "I'm so sorry," she said. "I can understand your feelings."

The clerk snatched her hand away. "How can you understand?" she asked, her voice seething with anger. "You are an American. You and your family never had to go through what we Latinos are going through because of this senator's prejudice against us."

"It's true, I never had to go through anything like this myself," Liz replied, "but I know something about prejudice against immigrants. My great grandparents came to the United States from Ireland at a time when the Irish were not welcome here. People treated them like scum. They could only get the most menial jobs and it was hard for them to find places to live. There were signs everywhere saying 'HELP WANTED, NO IRISH NEED APPLY' and 'ROOMS FOR RENT. NO IRISH WANTED.'"

The sales clerk looked surprised. "I did not know Anglos were ever treated like that in the United States."

Liz suppressed a smile. Her Irish ancestors would turn over in their graves if they heard someone refer to them as Anglos.

"Immigrants have always endured prejudice," she said. "But this new legislation Senator Ritchie pushed through is especially hard on your people. I'm sorry you're having trouble getting your mother and brother here. I hope it works out, soon."

"Thank you, you are very kind," the sales clerk said.

Suddenly her eyes and Liz's were locked in a penetrating gaze, and just as suddenly Liz sensed a feeling of mutual regard. She and this young woman could easily become friends, she thought. For a few moments she forgot why she'd come to Sohms.

"What's your name?" she asked.

"Angie Diaz. What is yours?"

"Liz. Liz Rooney."

They smiled at one another. In Angie's smile, Liz sensed a hunger for friendship. She must know very few people in New York.

"I like talking to you, Angie. I wish I wasn't so rushed, but I'm on my lunch break. I have to leave as soon as I buy the slip."

"I liked talking to you, too, Liz," Angie said.

"Maybe we could get together sometime soon."

Angie nodded. "I am off work at six. We could meet somewhere for coffee this evening if you are free."

She was right—Angie needed friends, Liz thought. "This evening will be fine," she said. They arranged to meet in a coffeehouse near Sohms.

"Well, I guess I'd better buy a slip and be on my way before I get fired from my job," Liz said with a laugh. She picked up one of the slips and nodded. "I'll take this one." She gave her credit card to Angie and waited while she rang up the sale.

"This is beautiful," Angie commented, folding the slip into a bag.

"I think so, too," Liz replied. "It's a birthday present for my mother."

"Oh, do you want to have it gift wrapped?" Angie asked.

That would mean taking the parcel someplace else in the store and waiting, Liz thought. "I wish I had time but I'm running late," she replied. Suddenly she noticed a strange expression on Angie's face.

"What's the matter, Angie?" she asked.

"Asking you if you wanted the slip gift wrapped made me remember something," Angie replied. For an instant, Liz thought that was all she intended to say, but after a pause she cast a furtive glance around to see if anyone was within earshot, and added. "I want to tell you something I have been keeping to myself because I am afraid."

Liz reminded herself she'd come to Sohms to get information and pass it along to Eichle. But now, on the brink of getting it, she knew she couldn't listen to what Angie had to say and then betray her confidence.

"Wait, Angie," she said. "Are you sure you want to confide in me? Until a few minutes ago I was a total stranger. Surely there's someone else you could tell."

Angie shook her head. "I have only one friend in New York. I have already told him about this, but there is more…" Her voice trailed off.

"Why don't you have other friends, Angie? There are many Hispanic organizations in the city where you could meet people."

"I did not come to this country to associate only with Hispanics," Angie replied. "I want to make friends with Anglos, too. I feel like we could be friends, Liz, and I want to tell you what is troubling me." She took a deep breath and lowered her voice. "Senator Ritchie was in here a few hours before he was murdered. I waited on him. He bought a black silk nightgown, size extra large."

"Was anyone with him?" Liz asked. She quelled her disappointment when Angie said the senator was alone. "You needn't be afraid to tell anyone about that, Angie," she said. "You haven't done anything wrong."

Suddenly Angie seemed close to tears. "Oh, Liz, there is so much I want to tell you…" She stopped abruptly as two women customers approached the counter.

"We both better get to work," Liz said, picking up her parcel. "I'll see you tonight at the coffeehouse, Angie, and we'll have a good talk. Six-fifteen. Okay?"

"Yes, okay," Angie replied.

Whatever Angie had to tell her, Liz sensed it might be something the police should know. She must explain this to Angie beforehand. She hoped this would not make Angie change her mind about confiding in her.

EICHLE PHONED LATE in the afternoon. "Can you meet me for a quick dinner around seven tonight?" he asked. "It's on me."

"Thanks, but it depends on where you want to eat," she said. "I have something to do in the Rockefeller Center area after work. If you want to meet somewhere near there I could make it around seven."

He mentioned one of the restaurants in Radio City Music Hall's underground area.

"That's not fast food," she said.

"I didn't mean that quick," he replied. "I'm working overtime on the Waldorf case, but we'll have time to talk about it. I want to fill you in on a couple of things we picked up today."

She never dreamed it would happen—Eichle treating her like a partner instead of a pariah!

She'd tell him about going to Sohms. She hoped he wouldn't resent this and revert to his old disapproving manner.

Her best friend, Sophie Pulaski, phoned just before quitting time. For the past few months Sophie had been a great source of information about homicide cases. She was a rookie cop, until lately in homicide reports and records, but now she'd been assigned to patrol and soon wouldn't be able to overhear and pass along information anymore. This could have been a bad blow to Liz as far as following homicides was concerned.

What luck that Eichle had suddenly become tolerant, even cooperative, of her interest in following murder cases. It couldn't have happened at a more opportune time.

"Sorry I don't have anything to report about the Waldorf murders," Sophie said. "I've been away from my desk getting briefed before I start on patrol. Mike Kovich is going to be my partner. He's been showing me the ropes."

"Well, I have something to report," Liz said. "You're not going to believe this, but Eichle has been letting me in on a few things concerning the case."

"The old grouch is giving you information? You're kidding!"

"It's true. He came over last night and let me look at two crime scene photos. We tossed a few ideas around about the case. I'm meeting him for a quick bite tonight and more talk."

"What got into Detective Pickle-Puss? Is he rewarding you for helping him solve the playboy poisoning?"

"I think so. Of course there's a lot he won't tell me."

"He should realize by now you know when to keep your mouth shut."

"I'm sure he does, or he wouldn't have told me anything at all. But that's enough about Eichle. When are we going to get together?"

"How about tomorrow after work? Meet you at the newsstand as usual." A teasing note came into Sophie's voice. "Unless you have another date with Eichle."

"Quit your kidding, Sophie. My meeting with Eichle tonight isn't a date. We're just going to have something to eat and exchange ideas about the case. He said he's working overtime on it and he'll have to eat and run."

"Well, whatever you want to call it, I hope you enjoy it," Sophie said. "I gotta go now. Mike just came in. See you tomorrow night."

"Can you wait a couple of minutes? I have something to tell you." She wanted to give Sophie a rundown on her encounter with Angie.

"Mike's breathing down my neck," Sophie replied. "You can tell me tomorrow."

Liz put down the phone with rueful sigh. After being inseparable since first grade, she and Sophie seemed to be heading in different directions. It wasn't only because Sophie had been assigned to patrol. She'd just become engaged and was going to be married in the fall. From now on their frequent meetings for coffee after work would be few and far between.

She thought of her meeting tonight with Angie.

Again, she sensed the potential for a friendship. If it did develop, it would help fill the void. *One door closes and another one opens...*

THREE

ON HER WAY TO MEET ANGIE, Liz passed a newsstand. She hadn't intended to pick up a copy of the *Daily News*. There wouldn't be anything in it she hadn't already heard on TV. The nightgown story was still limited information. The people at the *Informer* knew all about it, but their scandal sheet wouldn't hit the stands till tomorrow. But as she walked past the stand, the *News* headline caught her eye.

NIGHTIE BOUGHT FOR WALDORF TRYST

The daily tabloid had somehow managed to scoop the scandal sheet. How could this have happened? Who else could have found out about Senator Ritchie's fatal purchase? She bought a copy.

She read the story on the subway. The reporter had it all down; the gift wrapped box from Sohms, the nightgown, the size and the fact that it was much too large for the senator's wife. The article boldly suggested that the nightgown had been purchased for the senator's slain companion, "Nadine Berkman, a reporter for the *National Informer*." Only one thing was not included in the article—the fact that the nightgown was also too large for Nadine. That was because the *News* reporter, in his haste to scoop the *Informer*, hadn't done

his homework, Liz decided. He didn't know Nadine was
very slim. At least the *Informer* hadn't been scooped
one hundred percent. It would have its revenge when it
came out the next day.

Again, she wondered how the *Daily News* managed
to pull this off. One of their reporters must have been
in the Waldorf lobby when Senator Ritchie picked up
his parcel.

He'd seen Nadine approach the senator. He watched
them go up on the elevator. *Senator Spotless with a
young chick and a gift wrapped box bearing the distinc-
tive Sohms Fifth Avenue logo.*

But how did the reporter know what was in the box?
He must have phoned Sohms customer service, pretending to be from the store, saying he was checking up
on a parcel delivery for Senator Ritchie to make sure
the right merchandise had been sent out. The customer
service clerk assured him a black silk nightgown, size
extra large, had been delivered and signed for by the
senator. Angie must have written down on the receipt
what was in the box, along with the delivery address,
before it went to the gift-wrapping department. That
had to be what happened.

She wouldn't mention this to Angie. It would only
add to her distress.

AT THE COFFEEHOUSE, Liz got right to the point. "Before
you tell me what's on your mind, Angie, I must let you
know it might have to be passed on to the police."

Angie looked alarmed. Liz hastened to calm her.
"Nothing's going to happen to you. The police will be
grateful for any information you give them."

But the frightened expression on Angie's face intensified. For a moment Liz thought she was going to clam up, but then, almost in a whisper, she replied, "I am to blame for the murders at the Waldorf."

For a few seconds Liz was too startled to speak. "Why?" she asked.

Angie's words came bursting out, as if they'd been locked in her mind. "The nightgown Senator Ritchie bought was the kind a man buys for his wife or sweetheart. I knew it was not for his wife because I have seen her on TV and she is a very small woman, and the nightgown was an extra large size."

She paused, swallowing hard, as if to choke back rising tears. "Oh, Liz, I did a terrible thing. I wanted to shame the senator. I went to the *National Informer* with the sales receipt showing the nightgown was extra large. The woman I spoke to said it would make a good story. She paid me two hundred dollars…" Her voice broke. "And now the woman is dead, and the senator too."

Discussing criminal cases with Pop had taught Liz how to piece bits of information together. The woman who paid Angie the two hundred dollars and turned up dead in Senator Ritchie's hotel suite a few hours later had no intentions of using the nightgown story for publication. Instead she'd decided to blackmail the senator.

She explained it to Angie. "Don't blame yourself for that woman's death," she said. "She paid you for your information because she planned to use it to get money out of Senator Ritchie. That's why she went to the Waldorf."

Some of the anxiety drained away from Angie's face. "Then her death is not entirely my fault."

"You shouldn't blame yourself for the senator's death, either," Liz said. "You didn't know what was going to happen."

Angie gave a wan smile. "You have made me feel better, Liz, but there is more I must tell you." She lowered her voice. "I made another terrible mistake when I told my friend about Senator Ritchie and the nightgown and about selling my information to that paper."

Liz reached across the table and patted her hand. "The story will be in their next issue anyway. I think it comes out tomorrow."

"You do not understand," Angie said. "This person I told—this friend—he is a Puerto Rican Nationalist. He has great hatred for Senator Ritchie because the senator is against Puerto Rican independence." She paused, as if she could not bring herself to go on.

"Are you saying you think your friend might have something to do with the murders?" Liz asked.

"Yes," Angie replied, her voice trembling.

"When did you tell him about Senator Ritchie and the nightgown?"

"Yesterday. We met right here in this coffeehouse after I got off work."

That would have been shortly after six, Liz thought. "How long were you and your friend together last evening?" she asked.

"Not very long. He finished his coffee and said he had another appointment." She covered her face with her hands. "Oh, Liz, he left right after I told him the senator was staying at the Waldorf."

"Calm down, Angie. That doesn't mean he went to the Waldorf to shoot the senator." Liz said. "Do you truly believe he hates him that much?"

Angie nodded. "Juan has told me many times that Senator Ritchie is the leader of those in United States government who are against Puerto Rican independence. He says the senator wants to keep Puerto Rico under the thumb of the United States."

There wouldn't be any point in telling Angie that only a very small percentage of Puerto Rican people wanted independence, Liz decided. When Pop was on the force he'd made friends with many Puerto Ricans in Manhattan. He'd learned that in their recent elections, Puerto Ricans had three choices: independence, statehood or remaining a commonwealth under United States jurisdiction. They'd voted overwhelmingly for the status quo. Even statehood did not come close, and independence trailed well behind.

"The Nationalist movement went downhill after they tried to assassinate President Harry Truman back in the 1950s," Pop had told her. "There's not much left of it anymore except a few hotheads."

"Angie, your friend Juan enjoys almost all the rights and privileges of full United States citizenship. If Puerto Rico ever became an independent nation, that would end. The Puerto Rican people would have to go it alone. It would be very difficult."

"Juan told me there would be an alliance with Cuba and with some Arab countries who do not like the United States," Angie replied.

This Juan sounded like trouble, Liz thought. "Do you really think he's capable of murder, Angie?"

"I believe Juan would do anything to help his country break away from the United States," Angie said.

Eichle would be interested in this, Liz decided. "Angie," she said. "You must tell the police what you've told me."

Angie's eyes widened. Again, she looked frightened. "No, please, I cannot do that," she said.

Liz wondered, was Angie's fear for Juan, or did she think becoming involved with the police might further delay her efforts to bring her family into the country? "This would not affect your progress with Immigration, Angie," she said. "It might even count in your favor."

Some of the fear drained away from Angie's face. "But Juan—he will be arrested?" she asked.

"He'll be questioned but if it turns out he had nothing to do with the murders, of course he will not be arrested."

Angie sighed. "All right. I will tell the police about him. How will I do this, Liz? Shall I go to a police station?"

For a moment Liz thought about taking Angie with her to the restaurant to meet Eichle. She decided against it. Better to let Eichle know, beforehand, about Angie. He could take it from there.

"I know one of the police detectives who's working on the case," she said. "I'm meeting him for dinner tonight. I'll set something up."

Unexpectedly Angie smiled. "This policeman—he is your sweetheart?"

The question startled Liz. "Oh, no. Absolutely not," she replied. "He's just someone I've known for a while." She could have said Eichle was just a friend, but she wasn't sure if what they had going could be called friendship. She decided to change the subject.

"Tell me about yourself, Angie," she said.

"What is it you would like to know?" Angie asked.

"For starters, where did you live before you came to the States?"

"I was born and grew up in a small village in Colombia."

"Is that where your mother and brother live?"

"Yes."

Angie's father must have died, Liz thought. Since Angie had not mentioned this, she hesitated to ask. Instead she inquired about other relatives. "Do you have other family members there?"

Angie shook her head. "I have only my mother and youngest brother." Her face saddened. "My father and two other brothers are dead. They were killed by the rebels during the trouble a few years ago."

Liz was horrified. "Oh, Angie…"

To her surprise, Angie reached over and patted her hand. "Our life was not all sadness, Liz. When I was a young child it was good. We always had enough to eat. My father tended the gardens around the church and the rectory. My mother was well and strong then, and she was the padre's housekeeper. Padre Leon, his name was. He and a few nuns ran a school for the children of our village, Enough to teach us what you call in this country the three R's."

Angie must have had much more than the three R's, Liz thought. A moment later Angie confirmed this.

"When I reached the age when children left the church school, Padre Leon and the sisters wanted me to continue my education. They arranged for me to go to a convent school in Bogota. I did not want to go away from my family, but the sisters explained it was a wonderful opportunity that no other girl from our village had ever been given, and my father did not have to pay anything. I was awarded something they called *la beca*. I have forgotten the correct English word for this."

"I believe the word is scholarship," Liz said. The sisters and the priest had recognized rare intelligence in Angie, she thought.

Angie nodded. "Yes, scholarship. That is it."

"Was it hard for you to leave your family?"

"Yes. At first I was very homesick, but after a while I became accustomed to it and began to enjoy my studies. Never had I realized how much there was to learn." She paused with a rueful smile. "I am sorry. I am talking too much about myself."

"No you're not, Angie. Tell me more. How did you happen to come to the States?"

"This, too, is a long story."

"Please, go ahead and tell it."

"I will try and shorten it," Angie said. "I had been in the convent school nearly four years when the Mother Superior told me the wife of an American diplomat in Bogota had inquired about hiring a girl to help care for their baby daughter on weekends. The Mother asked me if I would be interested in such a job and I was. I had learned about the United States and I had become very interested. I knew this would be a chance to meet some Americans and experience how they lived."

Angie could not have been much more than a child, herself, at the time, Liz thought. She wondered how the diplomat and his wife had reacted when they first saw her.

As if Angie had read her mind, she laughed. "When the Americans came to interview me I could tell they did not want to hire me. Señora Miller told me I was too young to take care of a two-year-old, but after we talked awhile she agreed to try me out for one weekend."

Liz got the picture. Not only had Angie passed the weekend test, but she'd gone on to become a valued employee. "The Millers brought you to the States with them, didn't they?" she asked.

"Yes. The same year I finished my education at the convent school, Señor Miller—Mr. Miller—was transferred to Washington, D.C. In my home village, trouble with the rebels had been going on for several years. My father and two older brothers had been killed. Mama still had her job as housekeeper for Padre Leon. She and my one remaining brother moved to a smaller house and Hermano did not have to leave school and find work. Nevertheless, when the Millers asked me to go with them, I thought I should get a job in Bogota instead, to be closer to them. But the padre promised me that Mama would have her housekeeping job as long as she wanted it and he would keep a watchful eye on her and on Hermano until I could make arrangements for them to come to the United States."

"That sounds like a smooth plan. What went wrong?"

"First, Mama started feeling weak. Padre Leon's doctor examined her and said it was her heart and she must not do heavy housework anymore. Padre hired someone to do the heavy work and kept Mama for the light tasks, while still paying her the same money."

"Your Padre Leon sounds like a truly good man."

Angie's eyes grew moist. "Yes, he was good."

Liz noticed the trace of tears and the way she'd said *"was."* The priest must have died, she thought. If he had, she could imagine what took place after that.

Angie confirmed these thoughts. "The new padre did not have the interest in Mama and Hermano that Padre Leon had. He would not even pay Mama half as much. Mama wanted Hermano to stay in school, so they moved again, this time to a place where the houses are just shacks. When I got word of this I had been here for almost three years and Mr. Miller had just received a big promotion in the State Department and was going to be transferred to London."

"Being a big shot in the State Department, he could find a way for you to go with them, but I guess you wanted to stay here."

"Yes. I have grown to love this country. I had already decided I want to be an American citizen. When I told Mr. Miller this, he helped me change my immigration status. He helped me file for permanent resident status and get my green card so I could remain here after they left for London and be employed as something other than a child's nanny while I am waiting to apply for citizenship."

"How long before you can apply?"

"I will be eligible in about four years." Her face saddened. "If I were a citizen now, I would have a better chance of bringing Mama and Hermano in. Now that I know they are living in poverty I want this more than ever. Mama's heart is getting weaker. In her last letter she said she cannot work at all and Hermano has dropped out of school to find what jobs he can, but there is not much work except in the coca fields."

"After all the years your parents worked for the church, surely the priest will help them."

"Mama wrote that the sisters came twice with a basket of food." She frowned. "I have a good job and a nice apartment and I am able to take care of them, but, because of Senator Ritchie, their immigration has been delayed again and again."

"Where's your apartment, Angie?"

"On Staten Island."

"Staten Island! That's where I was born and lived all my life till my parents moved to Florida a few months ago. My grandmother still lives there."

"Then you must know the place where I live," Angie said. "It's St. George, right near the ferry. Was your home near St. George?"

"No, we lived in New Dorp. I have to take a train from the ferry when I go to visit my grandmother. With my parents in Florida, she's the only family I have nearby."

Angie's family was thousands of miles away, she thought. Suddenly it struck her that Angie might enjoy going with her to visit Gram sometime. "Maybe you'd like to go along next time I visit my grandmother," she said.

Angie's eyes lighted up. "Oh, Liz—I would like that very much. Could we go soon?"

"Sure. How about next Sunday?"

Angie nodded, smiling. "I do not work on Sundays so that would be fine."

"Okay. I'll check with Gram first and let you know."

"Thank you, Liz," Angie said, still smiling.

If the idea of going to visit someone's grandmother could excite Angie like this, she must not have much of a social life, Liz decided.

"You were going to give me your phone number for the detective, so you might as well give it to me now," she said. "I'll call you later tonight, after I've talked to Gram. If this Sunday isn't okay for her we'll set it up for another Sunday."

Angie provided her number. "Please give me yours, Liz," she said. She wrote it in a small notebook, saying, "Until now I have only such numbers as the electric and gas companies and the Bureau of Immigration."

"How about your friend Juan? Don't you have his phone number in there?"

"I did have, but I crossed it out. I do not think I can be friends with him anymore."

"Angie, you don't know for sure if he had anything to do with the murders," Liz said. At that moment she noticed a startled look on Angie's face.

"He is here, Liz—Juan—he just came in and he has seen us."

A moment later a tall, personable young man approached the table. He greeted Angie and eyed Liz.

"Hello Juan, meet my friend Liz," Angie said. Knowing her feelings about him, Liz was surprised she spoke so calmly.

A broad smile spread over Juan's face, revealing

white, even teeth. "I am pleased to meet you, Señorita Liz," he said, in a voice containing only a trace of Latino accent.

"I'm pleased to meet you too, Juan," Liz replied. Actually, she wasn't at all displeased. She'd been expecting some wild-eyed revolutionary type. This clean cut young man in a crisp white shirt and tan slacks didn't fit the role.

"We would ask you to join us but we were just going to leave," Angie said.

She rose from her chair. Liz had to get up, too.

With the suggestion of a bow, Juan smiled and said, "Adios, *señoritas*."

Leaving the coffeehouse, Angie looked over her shoulder to make sure he was not within earshot. "I hope you are agreeable to this, Liz," she said. "I had to get away from him. When I saw him come in I could think only that he might have committed the murders."

"It's okay. It was almost time for me to leave, anyway," Liz replied. How sad that Angie should suspect Juan of murder, she thought. There must have been something developing between them before all this happened.

They stood outside for a few minutes before Angie headed for the subway and Liz went to the restaurant to meet Eichle.

"I'll phone you tonight and let you know for sure about Sunday," Liz said.

"Thanks again for asking me," Angie replied. She smiled. "We are becoming real friends, Liz."

Liz returned the smile. "Yes, we are. And don't

forget, I'm going to give your phone number to the police detective." She glanced at her watch. "It's time I got going to meet him. I'll talk to you later, Angie."

FOUR

EICHLE WAS WAITING for her in the corridor outside the restaurant. "I guess you know the nightgown story's out in the *Daily News*," he said.

She nodded. "And tomorrow the scandal sheet will have the rest of it." Including the blackmail scheme, she thought. He didn't yet know that she'd figured out Nadine's reason for going to the Waldorf.

When they were inside and seated, she said, "The Extra Large Lady will know she's wanted for questioning. Too bad the size difference couldn't have been kept quiet."

"There's no way we could stop it. Even if the news hadn't broken the story, the *Informer* knows as much as we do and they're not going to sit on a story like that."

They wouldn't sit on the blackmail story, either, Liz thought. Was he going to tell her about that or would she have to let him know she'd figured it out?

"The scandal sheet will be published tomorrow," he said. "They'll spill everything they know. After that, the whole city will realize we're looking for Big Bertha."

Big Bertha. Catchy, but not quite the right label for a woman who probably could have been the favorite model of seventeenth-century painters. But at least Eichle was able to see some humor in the situation, even though the newspapers had foiled his chances of keeping the Rubenesque beauty under wraps.

"I have a couple of ideas for you to play around with," Eichle said, as they ordered their dinners—he, steak, medium rare with sautéed mushrooms, baked potato dolloped with sour cream, and a huge Caesar salad; she, poached salmon with lemon, potato soufflé, and a medley of green vegetables.

She still couldn't get used to him going along with her passion for solving murder cases. If, as Sophie had suggested, this was his way of rewarding her for providing an important clue in a recent case, then she didn't need to feel beholden to him. But, was this a one-shot kind of thing? When he felt he'd rewarded her enough, would he go back to telling her she shouldn't meddle in police business? She decided to make the most of his mellow mood while it lasted.

"Does that mean you're going to tell me how it went with Mrs. Ritchie today?"

"Right."

"So…?"

"She has an alibi that appears to be airtight. She says she was at home in her Washington apartment the evening of the murder. Her maid served her dinner around seven o'clock."

This wouldn't be the first time a loyal servant covered for an employer, Liz thought, and he'd said the alibi only *appeared* to be airtight. "Any other backups?" she asked.

"Washington police questioned the security guard and doorman on duty that afternoon. She was out of the building earlier and came back at 5:30 p.m."

That should eliminate Mrs. Ritchie as a suspect, Liz decided. *Unless she'd hired a hit man.* Maybe she'd known for years that her husband was not the saint he'd pretended to be. Maybe she'd reached the breaking point with his secret philandering and hypocrisy. But a hit man wouldn't leave his gun at the scene.

"Have you found anything about the gun registration?" she asked.

"We're still working on that," he replied.

As if to compensate for clamming up about the gun, Eichle reminded her he'd done some questioning at the *Informer* earlier in the day. "We were right about Nadine being in the wrong place at the wrong time," he said. "The managing editor didn't know anything about any interview with Senator Ritchie."

"So why was she in his room?" Liz asked, even though she knew. Would Eichle be straight with her and tell her about the blackmail plan?

"The managing editor said he was out of the office yesterday but we got some interesting answers from other employees." A lengthy pause followed this statement.

He enjoyed teasing her with bits of information, she thought. She'd had it with his cat and mouse games. "Did they mention a pretty, young woman coming in and talking to Nadine and Nadine writing her a check?" she asked.

He stared at her, his brow furrowing. "You went to Sohms, didn't you?" he asked. Without waiting for an answer, he gave an exasperated groan. "I should have known you were up to something when you asked me if the nightgown box had a store name on it. You talked to the sales clerk who waited on the senator, didn't you?"

"How else was I going to find out what happened at the *Informer?*"

"I would have told you. You didn't give me a chance."

"Oh, right, just like you were going to tell me why Nadine went to the Waldorf."

"Why do I get the feeling you've already figured that out?"

"Because I have. It was going to be a shakedown."

He gave a grudging grin. "You're pretty sharp, Rooney. Okay, so Nadine had blackmail in mind. I *was* going to tell you. No reason not to. Like I said, at the *Informer* they're wise to it and they're going to publish the story tomorrow."

"Do they have any evidence of a blackmail scheme?"

"Only that Nadine was seen talking to a young woman and writing her a check when the boss was out. But since when did that scandal sheet need hard evidence?"

"How about you? What evidence did you find at the scene?"

"We found a copy of the Sohms sales receipt on the floor and another when we searched Nadine's purse. Her checkbook was in there too."

"Had she recorded her check to Angie on the stub?"

"*Angie?* Sounds like you got chummy with the sales clerk."

"I did. So what about the stub?"

"There was a notation. A check was written Tuesday to an Angelita D. If you know her last name, you could save us some digging."

"It's Diaz." She was about to tell him she had Angie's phone number, but he surprised her with another statement.

"I might as well tell you we have another possible suspect. The *Informer* will be sure to come out with something on that tomorrow, anyway."

"Another suspect? Who?"

The waiter appeared with their dinners at that moment. Eichle waited till he'd gone before answering. "We found out from a friend of Nadine's at the newspaper that Nadine had a jealous boyfriend."

That would work, Liz thought. The jealous boyfriend could have tailed Nadine to the Waldorf and seen her go up in the elevator with the senator. But if he'd shot them, would he have been careless enough to leave his gun behind?

Eichle sliced into his steak and looked at her with the suggestion of a smile. "I know you're thinking about the weapon being left at the scene."

"I'm also thinking about you saying a woman would be more likely than a man to panic and run off without the weapon."

"From what we were told, this guy loses his cool when he gets jealous. He might have lost it again after he realized what he'd done." He glanced down at his plate. "This is great beef. How's your salmon?"

"Very good. Do you have the guy's name?"

"Nadine's friend at the paper told us his name and where he lives. Lou Sanchez and I were over there earlier but he wasn't home from work yet. Lou's parked outside the building now. He'll call me when the boyfriend shows up."

The jealous boyfriend angle sounded promising, Liz thought, but she had to tell him about Juan Vega. "So you now have three possible suspects," she said. "Mrs. Ritchie, if you're still counting her, the unidentified Big Bertha and Nadine's boyfriend. Would you like to try for four?"

"Does this have something to do with the Sohms sales clerk?"

"Yes. I had coffee with her before I came to meet you." She told him about Juan Vega.

"We haven't had anything on the Puerto Rican Nationalists for a long time," Eichle said. "But the FBI keeps on top of their activities. If anything was going on, the Bureau and the NYPD would cooperate in protecting the senator."

"So you don't think the Nationalists would have targeted the senator?"

"No. For one thing, he's not important enough."

"Angie says Juan detests him. He could have done this on his own."

"Sure, he could have, but would a calculating killer have left his gun at the scene?"

Liz nodded. "You're right. He didn't strike me as the panicky type." Another thought flashed into her mind. "But he could have used a stolen gun and left it behind to throw suspicion on the owner."

Eichle laughed. "Your pop's right, you'd make a good detective. Any chance of that happening?"

"No, I've never thought about joining the force," she replied. She would have told him she'd thought about becoming a private investigator someday, but she knew he'd react the same way Pop had. "Forget it, Lizzie," he'd said. With few expections, P.I.'s didn't get much respect from homicide cops. If she ever decided to take up that line of work she'd make sure she was one of the exceptions.

"Thanks for telling me about Vega, anyway," Eichle said.

He shouldn't brush Juan off so quickly, Liz thought. "Angie thinks Juan had something to do with the murders and she says she's to blame that they happened," she said.

That got his attention, just as she knew it would. "Why does she think she's responsible?" he asked.

"Because if it hadn't been for the nightgown information, Nadine wouldn't have gone to the Waldorf, and because she told Juan about it later and mentioned that the senator was staying at the Waldorf."

Eichle suddenly looked interested. "Sounds like she set the wheels in motion. I was going to drop in at Sohms tomorrow anyway to try and find this sales clerk and get her statement. Now that I have her name…"

"Please don't go to Sohms," Liz said. She explained Angie's situation with the Immigration Bureau and her fears that being questioned by the police might somehow interfere with her efforts to bring her mother and brother here. "Couldn't you interview her privately? I have her home phone number for you. She's expecting your call." She handed him a piece of paper with Angie's number on it.

He looked at it. "This isn't a Manhattan number. Looks like Staten Island."

"She lives in St. George."

"Tell you what. I'll have her come to the station house."

"That would be much better."

"Too bad she's having such a rough time with Immigration."

"She blames Senator Ritchie's legislation for that."

"Sounds like she has as much reason as her Puerto Rican friend for disliking Ritchie."

"Yes, she does, but don't even think about suspecting her. She wouldn't have gone to the *Informer* with the story if she intended to shoot the senator."

"She could have done that to rough up her tracks."

The idea of Angie on the list of murder suspects shocked Liz. "Angie couldn't have done such a terrible thing! When you meet her and talk to her, you'll know she's not a killer. She…"

"Chill out, Rooney. I'm kidding."

She wasn't altogether sure he was.

"How about dessert?" Eichle asked. Just as he spoke his cell phone sounded. "That'll be Lou," he said. After a few words he shoved the phone back in his pocket and signaled the waiter for the check.

"Nadine's boyfriend got home," Liz said.

"Right. I owe you a dessert, Rooney."

"I'd rather have a rundown on what happens with Nadine's boyfriend," Liz replied.

"We'll see," he said.

She watched him leave the restaurant. If Angie was on his list, that made five possible suspects, she thought. In all the homicide cases she'd followed, there'd never been so many.

On her own list, the unidentified size-large woman

was first. Eichle hadn't given so much as a hint which one was his own prime suspect. As she got up from the table, her mind teemed with speculation. If a police search was on to locate Big Bertha, maybe she was on the top of his list, too, and he was holding out on her.

These thoughts coursed through her mind as she left the restaurant. Just as she turned to walk towards the escalators, a man's voice sounded close behind her.

"We meet again, *señorita*."

An instant later Juan Vega fell into step beside her.

FIVE

THIS COULD NOT BE a chance encounter, Liz thought. He must have followed her to the restaurant after she left Angie and hung around till she came out.

"My apologies if I have startled you," he said.

Even in the midst of her uneasiness she noticed how well-spoken he was. "It's okay," she said. But, despite his cultured speech and courteous manner, it wasn't okay. His sudden appearance disturbed her.

"I was pleased to see you with Angie in the coffee-house," he said, as they stepped onto the escalator. "You were talking together like friends. This surprised me because I know Angie has kept to herself since she came to New York. I am the only friend she has here."

"I know—she told me," Liz replied. "She also told me about the trouble she's having trying to get her mother and brother here, because of Senator Ritchie's bill." As she spoke, she cast him a sharp glance. If he had anything to do with the Waldorf murders, the mention of the senator's name might stir a reaction.

It didn't.

"Ah, yes, the late, lamented senator," Juan said. He did not have to say "anti-Hispanic senator." The words were in his wry smile.

They reached the street level and went out onto the sidewalk. When he continued to walk along with her,

her uneasiness increased. While she was pondering how she could get rid of him she decided to ask him something she'd wondered about. "Do you know why Senator Ritchie is so prejudiced against Latinos?" she asked.

"Because of drug smuggling," he replied. "He had been trying to keep Hispanics out of this country ever since his nineteen-year-old daughter died of an overdose of crack cocaine at a college party."

"I didn't know about that," Liz said.

"It didn't make the national news because it happened before he became a senator. That's why he decided to run for the senate. He held Hispanic immigrants responsible. He was determined to keep out as many of them as possible."

"But that's unreasonable," Liz said.

"Senator Ritchie stopped being reasonable when his daughter died. It is unfortunate that Angie's mother and brother live in an area of Colombia where most of the people depend on the coca crop for their living."

"Oh, sure, like a sick mother and a young boy would be mixed up with drug smugglers," Liz retorted.

"If it were not for the coca crop there would be no drug trade," Juan said. "Angie's brother is no longer a little boy. He is almost thirteen. He and their mother depend on whatever work he can get."

He didn't need to elaborate. The economy of the village was dependent on the coca crop. Where else would Angie's brother find work? This didn't look encouraging for Angie's hopes.

"Are you on your way home?" Juan asked.

"Yes, I'm going to hail a cab." She hoped one would

come along soon. What he'd told her had been enlightening, but now she wanted to distance herself from him.

"Allow me," he said. He stepped to the edge of the sidewalk and gave a piercing whistle. Almost instantly a taxi swooped out of the stream of traffic and pulled up at the curb.

"Thanks," she said, getting in.

"My pleasure, *señorita*."

She raised her hand in a gesture of goodbye as he closed the cab door.

"Where to, lady?" the driver asked.

"Gramercy Park," she replied. She waited till the cab drew away before giving him the street and number. Juan might overhear. She didn't want him showing up at her door.

She told herself to cut the paranoia. By the time the cab stopped in front of her building she'd almost convinced herself it had been a chance encounter. Why would a Puerto Rican Nationalist want to follow her?

As she let herself into her apartment, another question popped into her mind. Should she tell Eichle about this? No, she decided. It had nothing to do with the case.

She got out of her clothes and into her pajamas and robe. It had been a productive evening, she thought, curling up on the sofa bed. Her meeting with Angie had drawn them closer into a friendship and dinner with Eichle had taken her further into the Waldorf case. Remembering what he'd said about Angie, she frowned. Did he suspect she had something to do with the murders, or had he been joking?

Thinking of Angie reminded her to call Grandma McGowan about a visit this Sunday. Grandma picked up on the second ring. "Oh. I'm glad you called now, dear," she said. "Another few minutes and I'd have gone out for the evening."

Liz had to smile. Gram's social life was way ahead of hers. She hadn't had a real date since her breakup with Wade a few weeks ago. Too bad he'd turned out to be such a drag about her interest in homicides. Unfeminine, he'd called it. Well, someday she'd meet a man who'd understand. Meanwhile, she was in no hurry.

"Where are you going tonight, Gram?" she asked. "Out with that man from church again?"

"Yes, he's picking me up to play cards with friends. What have you been up to, dear? I guess you've been following the Waldorf murders."

"Of course," Liz replied. Gram liked to follow homicide cases as much as she did. She hoped to get her input on this one, Sunday. "Gram," she said, "if you're not busy this Sunday I'd like to come and see you and bring a friend."

"Come for lunch," Gram replied. "Is this friend a new man in your life?"

Gram knew about Wade. "I'm glad you broke it up," she'd said. "He sounds like the controlling type."

She told Gram she was bringing a new woman friend. "She's from South America. I know you'll like her."

"I always enjoy your friends, dear," Gram said. "Oh, there's the doorbell. I must go. I'll see you and your friend around noon on Sunday."

Sunday was only two days away. By that time Eichle would have met with Angie. He would also have questioned Nadine's boyfriend. He'd have plenty to tell her next time he decided to give her a break.

Before she phoned Angie she turned on the TV news to catch the latest on the murders. Something should come on about Nadine's jealous boyfriend, she thought. Though he seemed a likely suspect, Ms. Extra Large was at the top of her list, with Mrs. Ritchie, alibi and all, second.

The newscaster was finishing a rehash of the nightgown story. Suddenly her voice took on a different tone. "Just in—this late-breaking development in the Waldorf murders. According to coworkers at the *National Informer,* female victim Nadine Berkman had a jealous boyfriend."

The way she said it, Liz could picture the boyfriend following Nadine to the Waldorf and confronting her with the senator.

"The boyfriend, Kurt Gerhardt, an electronic technician, is being questioned tonight by police," the newscaster said.

With the jealous boyfriend now all over the news, the blackmail story remained the sole unreported angle. It would probably be out in the next issue of the *Informer.*

"Stand by for live coverage at the residence of Kurt Gerhardt, boyfriend of Waldorf murder victim Nadine Berkman," the newscaster announced. A picture appeared on the screen showing reporters and TV camera crews gathered in front of an apartment building. A police squad car was visible in the background.

Again the newscaster announced that Gerhardt was being questioned by police. Meanwhile, nothing was happening. To fill the void, information about him was repeated.

Again, according to Nadine's coworkers, he was extremely jealous. The way the newscaster said "extremely," she might just as well have said "insanely," Liz thought. The scene was poised for the appearance of Kurt Gerhardt being led out of the building in handcuffs.

Suddenly the apartment door opened. Liz saw Eichle and Sanchez come out, fending off reporters as they made their way to their vehicles. Two uniformed cops followed and got into their squad car. That was it.

The crowd of reporters and onlookers voiced their disappointment with a roar of disapproval followed by a volley of questions.

"Why wasn't the boyfriend arrested?"

"Is he still under suspicion?"

"Where was he the night of the murders?"

A camera zoomed in on Eichle. He didn't look at all disappointed, Liz thought. Had he decided even before the questioning that the killer was not Kurt Gerhardt? Was this because he'd targeted Ms. Extra Large as his prime suspect?

"The department will issue a statement tomorrow," Eichle said, getting into his car.

The coverage ended with the newscaster advising viewers to stay tuned to the channel for further bulletins.

Liz turned the TV off and picked up the phone to call Angie. "I talked to my grandmother and we're on for Sunday," she said.

"We are on. This means we will go to visit her?" Angie asked.

Liz smiled. Angie's English was so good that it was easy to forget she wasn't into American slang. "Gram's delighted we're coming," she replied.

They arranged to meet at the St. George ferry terminal at 11:30 a.m. on Sunday. They'd hop the SIRT and be at Gram's by noon.

"Have you been watching TV, Angie?" Liz asked.

"Yes. Everyone knows about the nightgown now but not about the blackmail. And I heard Nadine Berkman had a jealous boyfriend and the police questioned him, but did not arrest him. The detective who spoke to the reporters—he is the one who is going to phone me?"

"Yes. His name's George Eichle. There'll be another detective with him when he questions you. Lou Sanchez. He's Cuban-American." Angie might feel more comfortable with another Latino present, she thought.

"This George Eichle, he has a good face," Angie said. "I do not think he will make me feel afraid."

Liz would not have described Eichle's face as good, but now that she thought about it, it wasn't all that bad. Anyway, she was sure he'd be kind to Angie. Nobody knew better than she that he could be a grouch, but that was because he resented what he called "meddling in police matters." He wouldn't try to intimidate Angie.

Suddenly she recalled her encounter with Juan Vega. Should she tell Angie about it? No, she decided. Angie was already upset and suspicious of him. Why upset her more?

"Call me after your questioning and let me know how it went," she said, before they rang off.

Tomorrow would be an interesting day, she thought, as she opened the sofa bed for the night. Besides Angie's report on her meeting with the police there was a chance Eichle might loosen up and tell her the details about Nadine's boyfriend. She and Sophie would have plenty to talk about when they met after work.

SIX

THE NEXT MORNING LIZ turned the TV on to a rehash of the black nightgown and jealous-boyfriend coverage. Also, police had come out with a statement that Kurt Gerhardt had an alibi. Fellow employees had backed up his claim that he'd been working till after 8:00 p.m. on the day of the murders and could not have tailed Nadine to the Waldorf.

Suddenly the newscaster announced a late-breaking story. Nadine's blackmail scheme was revealed. To counter yesterday's scoop by the *Daily News*, the *Informer* must have put out an early edition and the TV news had picked up on it, Liz decided.

She was right. A shot of the scandal sheet's front page came on. Bold headlines took up most of it.

SHAKEDOWN SCHEME IN WALDORF MURDERS

Below was a photo of Senator Ritchie at a recent political fundraiser and one of Nadine which looked as if it had been taken at an *Informer* Christmas party.

The newscaster read excerpts from the covering article, written in the scandal sheet's loose style. The slain reporter was referred to simply as "Nadine."

Quoting from the article inside, the newscaster stated

that Nadine was first thought to have gone to the Waldorf to rendezvous with the senator but police now believe she went there to blackmail him. "Evidence indicates Nadine was tipped off that the nightgown found at the murder scene was not purchased for the senator's wife," the newscaster said. "The nightgown was a size extra large. The senator evidently intended it as a gift for a woman much larger than Mrs. Ritchie. Though not as petite as Mrs. Ritchie, Nadine would have worn a small size."

The newscaster concluded by saying the woman for whom the senator had purchased the nightgown would be well over average height and weight.

This last statement could not have been a direct quote from the *Informer,* Liz thought. Their reporters would have described Ms. Extra Large as "full-blown" and "well-endowed." There might also have been a reference to Mae West.

Coverage of the nightgown story ended. Another newscaster came on to review the jealous-boyfriend angle.

"Police interrogated Nadine's boyfriend Kurt Gerhardt last night but failed to make an arrest," the newscaster announced. This sounded like a direct quote from the scandal sheet, Liz thought. She knew she was right when the newscaster read statements from *Informer* staff members.

"Nadine was trying to break up with her boyfriend because of his jealous rages," one coworker stated. "She recently moved out of their apartment and got her own place, but he wouldn't leave her alone. He was, like, stalking her all the time."

Listening to statements made by other employees, Liz began to notice a trend developing. Coverage of the jealous boyfriend was being played up while Nadine's blackmail scheme was being played down. It was clear that the staff of the *Informer* believed that Kurt Gerhardt should have been arrested and charged with the murders.

Time to leave for work. Reluctantly, she turned the TV off.

She stopped at a newsstand near her office and got a copy of the *Informer*. Before continuing on her way, she glanced at the front page of the *New York Times*. Evidently it had come out before the *Informer*. There was no mention of the nightgown or the blackmail scheme. The only coverage of the murders stated that police had questioned a male friend of the female murder victim last night but no arrest had been made.

When she got to the office she turned the TV news channel on for a few minutes while her computer was booting up. A different newscast was on, but the reporting was the same as before. The material had come straight out of the *Informer*. The scandal sheet was slanted in sympathy with Nadine. It was as if her plan to shake down the senator was justified because she needed the money to get away from Gerhardt. She was not only a murder victim but also the victim of a man whose intense jealousy drove her to do what she did. She had to get away from him. Even if he hadn't committed the murders they never would have happened if she hadn't been desperate for money. It was all his fault.

Just as Liz was about to turn off the TV in disgust,

a bulletin came on. Reporters had contacted Nadine's family in Oklahoma. Liz braced herself for more white-washing. Instead, she was almost pleased to hear that Nadine was not the misunderstood victim the *Informer* was making her out to be. Her parents were interviewed. They didn't appear at all shocked or saddened about their daughter's murder. They were quoted as stating she'd been estranged from the family more than six years. She'd left the small farming community where they lived and they hadn't heard a word from her since. As far as they were concerned she was already dead.

Why were they so bitter? Liz wondered. Families were usually forgiving when a prodigal died. An inter-view with a dour-faced aunt provided the answer.

"Nadine was a wayward girl who gave her parents nothing but trouble," she stated. "When she ran away she stole all the money her mother kept in the soup tureen on the top shelf in the kitchen—money she was saving for a new washing machine—and cleaned out the cash register in her father's grain and feed store. Everyone in town knew she'd come to no good end."

In response to questions about arrangements for trans-porting the body to Oklahoma for a funeral, Nadine's aunt admitted that such plans were being made by family members, adding, "Nadine was a bad girl but she was still kin."

ON HER LUNCH BREAK Liz went to a place with a TV behind the counter. The manager kept it tuned to the news channel. She got there just in time to see a shot of a Fifth Avenue apartment building and hear the newscaster say this was where Senator Ritchie's widow was staying with friends. Mrs. Ritchie had arrived in Manhattan Wednesday evening, the newswoman said. Since then she had been in seclusion except when the police questioned her on Thursday morning.

Surely she would have gone to view her husband's body, Liz thought. Maybe she'd given the reporters the slip Wednesday night by disguising herself. Or, on second thought, maybe she wasn't in any hurry to view the remains of the man who'd betrayed and humiliated her.

But she couldn't stay holed up forever, Liz thought. She would have to leave the building sometime. The media was counting on that. Camera crews and reporters were already gathered in front of the building.

She was halfway through her sandwich when the newscaster announced that Mrs. Ritchie had come out of the building. Cameras zoomed in on her as she made her way to a waiting car, accompanied by a young woman and an older man.

Liz could hear reporters shouting questions. *Barbarians,* she thought. Intense as her interest in murder cases was, she believed the bereaved should be allowed peace and privacy.

The man with Mrs. Ritchie must be a relative, either of her or the senator, she decided. Was the young woman her daughter? Then she recalled Juan saying that the Ritchie's only child had died.

A moment later the newscaster voiced speculation that Mrs. Ritchie might be on her way to arrange for the transportation of the senator's body to Massachusetts. "Accompanying her is the senator's brother, Lester Ritchie. The woman with her has not yet been identified."

Liz got a good look at the two women as they walked to the car. Mrs. Ritchie looked very small and anything but fashionable in a dark, outdated suit and a large, black, floppy brimmed hat. Maybe she thought the hat would shield her face and keep her from being identified. Instead, it only drew attention.

Her unidentified female companion had on a trendy gray jacket and pants outfit. She was bareheaded—a good-looking blonde, in her mid-thirties, Liz judged. Next to Mrs. Ritchie she appeared very tall. Further appraisal showed she was as tall as the senator's brother. Statuesque would describe her perfectly, Liz thought.

Statuesque enough to wear an extra large nightgown!

Who was she? If she were a relative, the media would probably have known. Maybe she was a member of the senator's staff who'd flown up from Washington with Mrs. Ritchie, or maybe she was Mrs. Ritchie's personal secretary. Many wives of prominent government figures had secretaries to schedule social events.

Eichle would know. He must have met her when he went to question Mrs. Ritchie yesterday. He couldn't have overlooked her physical proportions. He was too sharp not to have made the connection, yet he hadn't said a word about it at dinner last night. That could mean he thought the big blonde might be Ms. Extra Large but he didn't want to share his suspicions. With newscasters putting out the word that the nightgown was purchased for a woman built more like a Venus De Milo statue than a Barbie doll, how long did he think this could be kept quiet? Half of New York City's TV viewers would already have seen the amply-stacked blonde live onscreen, and the other half would see her in reruns.

On her way back to the office she noticed the *Daily News* being unloaded at the newsstand. She paused for a look at the front page. The headline was typical:

NIX NADINE NIGHTIE

The *New York Post* was also out. In lieu of headlines, its front page consisted of a large photo of a black nightgown superimposed with a huge white question mark. Liz knew the actual nightgown was stashed at police headquarters with other evidence in the case, but half the readers would assume this was it.

Curious to see how the *News* had handled the blackmail story, she bought a copy and read some of it while walking back to the office. Unlike the *Informer,* the *News* did not attempt to justify Nadine's scheme. At her desk she read the rest of the coverage and looked at photos of Nadine, evidently obtained from Oklahoma.

She'd just set aside the paper and was about to get to work when a voice startled her. "If you're done with your copy of the *News,* could I have a look at it?" Her temporary boss, Dr. LeRoy Jackson, filling in while Dan was on vacation, stood in the doorway.

"Sure, Dr. Jackson," she replied. She picked up the tabloid and handed it to him. This was the first time they'd spoken about anything other than work. She'd believed him to be rather standoffish.

"Thanks, I'll return it to you," he said. He paused, looking at her with a grin. "I hear you like to follow murder cases. This one's a puzzler, isn't it?"

"Yes…" Dan must have told him she was hooked on homicides. He didn't seem disapproving. Maybe she'd missed the boat, thinking he wouldn't let her in on forensic findings the way Dan did. About the gunshots, for example. Final reports had not been released for the computer. All she knew was what she'd seen in the photos Eichle had shown her. Dan would have already told her what kind of gun it was and how many shots had been fired. He would also have told her if he believed there'd been a struggle for possession of the gun.

Nothing ventured, nothing gained, she thought. "May I ask you something about the case, Doctor?" she asked.

"Sure."

"Could there have been a struggle for the gun? Could it have gone off when the victims tried to get it away from the killer?"

"I guess it could have happened that way," he replied.

She suppressed an exasperated sigh. To get a satisfactory answer she'd have to wait for the final forensic reports to reach her desk, or for Dan to return from vacation, whichever came first.

ANGIE PHONED DURING the afternoon to say she'd met with Eichle at the station house before going to work that morning. "Both he and the other detective were very kind to me," she said. "They did not make me feel ashamed for selling my information to that paper. The questions they asked were mostly about Juan. I did not like telling them that he left the coffeehouse soon after I told him Senator Ritchie was staying at the Waldorf, but

I had to be truthful. Afterwards, the tall Anglo with the good face who is your friend, he said he had to drive up Fifth Avenue anyway and he dropped me off at Sohms so I would not be late for work. He is very nice, Liz."

Liz's mind went on alert. Mrs. Ritchie was staying with friends on upper Fifth Avenue. Was that where Eichle was going—to question Mrs. Ritchie again? She set the idea aside while she concluded her talk with Angie.

"I'm glad everything went well at your interview. I was sure it would. Now that you've told the police what you know about Juan, you have nothing to worry about," she said.

"Unless Juan finds out I went to the police station," Angie said. "If he does find out, he will know the police questioned me and he will know I told them about him."

"How's he going to find out—and what if he did?" Angie didn't reply.

"Surely you're not afraid of him, are you, Angie?"

"Oh, no—at least I never was, before, but now…" Her voice trailed off. "I must go. I have customers," she said. "I will see you Sunday at the ferry terminal."

"RALPH'S ON DUTY TONIGHT, so how about having dinner and taking in a movie?" Sophie asked, when they met after work.

"Fine," Liz replied. Their once frequent dinners and movies had tapered off since Sophie started dating Ralph. He was a cop from another precinct—a great guy. Now they were making wedding plans, and Liz only got together with Sophie when Ralph was working late.

"I have some information for you," Sophie said, as they headed for their favorite after-work eating place. "I happened to see Eichle and Sanchez talking to a young Hispanic woman today. Looked like she was being questioned."

"I know about that," Liz said. She told Sophie about going to Sohms, about becoming friends with Angie, and about Juan Vega.

Sophie laughed. "You're some piece of work, Liz. When you decide to become a private eye, I'll quit the force and be your partner. Do you believe this Angie and her Puerto Rican boyfriend had anything to do with the Waldorf murders?"

"Not Angie. And I don't believe Eichle thinks she had anything to do with them either. I don't know what he thinks about Juan, but I'm sure he'll be questioned next."

"What do *you* think about this Juan?" Sophie asked. "Other than wanting to overthrow the Puerto Rican government, does he seem like an okay kind of guy?"

Liz recalled Juan's nice appearance and good manners. "He seemed okay, except…" She told Sophie about her encounter with him in Rockefeller Center. "But that could have been by chance," she added.

"What did Eichle say about it?"

"I didn't tell him. It doesn't have anything to do with the case."

"Maybe you'd better tell him anyway."

"I don't want him getting the idea I need his protection." Just thinking about that made her want to change the subject. "Did you see Mrs. Ritchie on TV today?"

"No. Anything interesting?"

"Yes. There was an unidentified young woman with her—a good-looking blonde."

Sophie caught the idea. "A big gal?"

"Big enough to fill out an extra large size nightgown."

"No kidding. And the TV news didn't know who she is?"

"Nope. But I'll bet Eichle knows. He must have met her when he went to question Mrs. Ritchie again."

"Didn't he mention her last night?"

"Not one word. He's holding out on me. He's been closemouthed about the murder weapon, too."

"I heard him talking with Lou Sanchez about the gun. It sounded like they're having trouble tracing the registration."

"Pop told me serial numbers can be filed off guns," Liz said. She made a mental note to ask Eichle next time she saw him if that's what happened to the Waldorf murder weapon. If there was a next time. She didn't know when he'd decide he'd shown her enough appreciation for helping him solve his last case.

"A hit man might use a gun with serial numbers filed off," Sophie said.

Liz nodded. "I thought of a hit man when I suspected Mrs. Ritchie and I was trying to figure out how she could have pulled it off, but a hit man wouldn't have left his gun at the scene."

"Unless it was someone else's gun."

Liz thought of her conversation with Eichle about

Juan. They'd agreed that he wouldn't have left his gun at the scene, either, and then she'd said it might have been a stolen gun.

Juan...Mrs. Ritchie...Ms. Extra Large...she shook her head. "There are so many possible suspects in this case, I'm getting confused."

"You need a break," Sophie said. "A good movie will fix you up. Let's decide which one."

SEVEN

NOT HAVING TO WORK on Saturdays meant not setting the alarm clock the night before, eating what Mom called a decent breakfast, doing laundry and cleaning the apartment. The laundry and cleaning never took very long. While her double-decker washer/dryer was sloshing behind the screen she'd set up to hide it, along with the kitchenette, she ran the vacuum cleaner around the rest of the apartment. Its one room wasn't much bigger than her bedroom in the house where she grew up.

Her parents still worried about her living alone in Manhattan, and in such a tiny apartment, Liz thought as she ran the duster attachment over the windowsills. Sure, it was small, but at least she could glimpse part of Gramercy Park from the windows. Besides, she didn't need any more space than this. She was pleased with the way she'd fixed it up. Furnishings from the Staten Island house gave her a sense of being home. And the landlord, Mr. Moscaretti, who doubled as superintendent, was friendly and obliging. He and his wife were about Mom and Pop's age. They lived directly below her on the ground floor of a nineteenth-century brownstone they'd converted into four apartments. Mrs. Moscaretti was a jolly woman who called her "dearie" and cajoled her husband into allowing her to install a washer and

dryer. "But if it leaks you pay the damages," they'd
warned.

Pop had sized them both up and decided she'd be
safe in their building, even if it wasn't equipped with
a buzzer entry system. The ink was barely dry on the
lease before he was calling them Joe and Rosa and they
were calling her parents Frank and Marge. It wouldn't
surprise her if Pop had asked the Moscarettis to keep
an eye on her, she thought, switching off the vacuum
cleaner. Not that she'd ever given her parents any real
trouble. If they'd believed she might start living a wild
life in the big city they'd have quit worrying by now.
There'd been no noisy parties, and her only male visi-
tors had been the recently dumped Wade, and Eichle.
Wade had always been very proper (most likely because
he knew her father was a cop) and Eichle was only
rewarding her for her help with his last case by feeding
her crumbs of information about this one.

It all added up to a tame existence. Tame but not
boring, she thought, putting the vacuum cleaner away
in a closet. Life would never be boring as long as there
were homicide cases to follow.

Thinking about her parents reminded her that
Wednesday was Mom's birthday and she hadn't mailed
the slip yet. But it was wrapped and ready to go. She'd
mail it today. There was one of those mail places not
far from her apartment.

Earlier she'd had the TV on in hopes of catching
something new in the Waldorf case. She'd turned it off
while cleaning because the vacuum made so much noise
she couldn't hear anything anyway. Now she switched it
on again, just in time to hear that police had questioned

another man last night. Even before the name was announced, she knew the man had to be Juan Vega.

She listened to the newscaster say that Juan Vega had ties to the Puerto Rican Nationalists, an organization known to be hostile towards Senator Ritchie. He'd been released after questioning. A photo of Juan was shown. Again, Liz thought, he didn't fit the revolutionary stereotype.

"Police had no further comment about Vega's questioning or about the recent questioning of Kurt Gerhardt, boyfriend of murder victim Nadine Berkman," the newscaster said. A photo of Gerhardt was shown. A blond, Teutonic type, Liz thought. Like a character in an old World War II movie. He could have played the part of a Gestapo agent.

No mention was made of Angie's interview. For this Liz was thankful. Eichle was okay after all. He'd decided Angie wasn't a suspect and letting the media know she'd been interviewed would serve no purpose.

Suddenly her senses went on alert. The newscaster was saying something about the Sohms Fifth Avenue sales clerk who'd sold the nightgown to Senator Ritchie.

With growing concern, Liz listened to the report. "According to murder victim Nadine Berkman's co-workers at the *National Informer,* the sales clerk at Sohms who sold Senator Ritchie the nightgown came into the newspaper office a few hours before the murder and presented proof to Nadine that the nightgown was three sizes larger than what the senator's wife wore. She was paid for her information."

Liz scarcely heard the newscaster quote the *Informer*'s

slant on Nadine's blackmail scheme. She could think only of Angie and her reaction to this. If she'd heard about it she must be terribly upset. Worse, she might lose her job.

But the report about Angie hadn't been on the most watched early news and her name hadn't been given in this latest one. The *Informer* didn't have it. She'd given Eichle Angie's last name herself and he hadn't released it. Good, she thought. She had some time. There was a chance none of the powers-that-be at Sohms knew about this yet. Most likely Angie didn't either. She decided to go to the store right away. She wanted to prepare Angie for the inevitable trouble to come and be there for her when it happened.

She rushed to change out of the old jeans and shirt she always wore when she cleaned the apartment. Dressed in a dark blue pants suit and white turtleneck sweater, she grabbed her purse and left. She was on the subway when she remembered Mom's birthday package. She'd have to mail it later.

SHE WAS RELIEVED to find Angie at her counter, busy with a customer. She didn't look at all distraught. Apparently nothing had happened yet.

Angie smiled when she saw her. "I will be right with you, miss," she said. She finished wrapping the customer's purchase and wished her a good day. Besides being very smart, Angie had a winning manner, Liz thought. The combination was all too rare among today's service employees. She prayed Sohms management would take this into consideration.

"Liz!" Angie said. "I did not expect to see you today.

I hope you have not come to tell me we are not going to visit your grandmother tomorrow."

"No, nothing like that. I need to tell you something. It's very important. Can you take a few minutes off?"

"Yes," Angie replied. She called across the aisle. "Shondra, I am taking a short break. Will you cover for me?"

"Sure," came the reply.

The woman's restroom was crowded. Liz told Angie they couldn't have a private conversation there. Angie suggested going to the stairwell.

"Nobody will hear us here," she said, as they stood in the small space between staircases. "What do you have to tell me that is so important?"

Liz told her about the news broadcast. "Your name wasn't given," she said. "The newspaper doesn't have it, but when word gets around about a Sohms sales clerk selling information to the *Informer,* it will only be a matter of time before store executives track you down."

Angie grew pale. Her eyes widened in shock. "I will lose my job," she managed to say.

Liz didn't try to tell her it might not happen. The more she thought about it, the more certain she became that an employee who'd sold information about a Sohms customer to a scandal sheet would be fired.

"What am I going to do, Liz?" Angie asked "I will lose my job and the store might not give me a reference. I will never be able to get another good job."

An idea flashed into Liz's mind. "Angie, I think you should go to the personnel office right now and talk to someone there about this. Is there anyone in that department you feel you could confide in?"

Angie nodded. "Gloria Sandoval. She has been the head of personnel for many years. She is a nice older lady who has taken an interest in me. Do you believe I should tell her what I have done?"

"Yes. She's going to find out, anyway. Telling her first will work to your advantage. Does she know about your problem with Immigration since Senator Ritchie's legislation?"

"Yes. She knows how worried I am about Mama and Hermano. She has been very kind and sympathetic."

"Then she'll understand you wanted to get even with Senator Ritchie and you also saw this as a chance to get some money for your family. If she realizes how you regret doing this, she might put in a good word for you with the higher-ups. What have you got to lose? Go and see her right now, Angie."

"But I told Shondra I would only be gone for a few minutes."

"I'll clear it with Shondra and I'll help her with customers. I worked two summers in a department store. I know how to run a register."

"I will get into trouble, letting someone who is not an employee take over my job."

Liz had to laugh. "Angie, you're already in trouble. This isn't going to make any difference. Go, now. I'll wait for you." She patted Angie's shoulder. "And good luck."

When Liz told Shondra that Angie would be away from her counter longer than expected, Shondra was curious and concerned.

"Is she sick or something?"

"No, she went to the personnel office. I'm going to wait for her here. If it gets busy I'll help."

"The personnel office? Is she quitting and are you taking her place?"

"No. I'm just going to wait for Angie but like I said, if it gets busy…"

"Okay, but the floor manager better not catch you."

"Would he have me arrested for impersonating a Sohms sales clerk?"

Shondra grinned. "If I see him coming, you can pretend you're a customer."

More than half an hour passed with no sign of Angie. The department got busy. Liz waited on several customers and made the sale every time.

"You're pretty good at this," Shondra said, during a lull. "Do you have some sort of selling job?"

"Far from it. I work for the medical examiner."

"The guy who does the autopsies? Do you help him with the dead people?"

"No. I have a desk job. Mostly, I handle computer records and correspondence." Since Shondra seemed interested, she added, "But I often go to murder scenes with my boss."

"No kidding. Did you go to the Waldorf after that senator and that woman were murdered?"

"No. My boss has been on vacation."

"I guess you heard that the senator bought the black nightgown here only a few hours before he was shot?"

Liz nodded. "Angie told me."

"Everyone here is talking about it. Imagine that

woman finding out the nightgown was too large for the senator's wife and deciding to blackmail him, and then walking right into her own murder."

It was hard for Liz to believe Shondra and the other sales clerks in Lingerie hadn't connected Angie to Nadine's blackmail scheme. Had the many possible suspects and different angles clouded the picture? She recalled her own feelings of confusion yesterday. But before this day ended, Shondra and everyone else at the store would know about Angie's involvement. Because the *Informer* did not know Angie's name, and the police—thanks to Eichle—had not revealed it, the general public would not immediately know the identity of the sales clerk who'd tipped off Nadine. But the sales clerk story would be repeated on the news all day. The people at Sohms Fifth Avenue would put it all together as soon as they heard the story.

Shondra's voice came into her thoughts. "What's keeping Angie? It's been almost an hour and we're getting busy again."

Several women converged around Shondra's counter. A few more were looking through the hangers of negligees and robes. While Shondra and the other clerks attended to these customers, Liz noticed a man heading towards Angie's counter. She turned and walked over to where he stood, looking into the showcase.

"May I show you something, sir?" she asked. Though the man's back was turned and she couldn't see his face, he had a youthful build. A young husband looking for an anniversary present, she thought.

The man turned around. She held back a gasp. There

was no mistaking the Teutonic face she'd seen on TV this morning.

Kurt Gerhardt's pale blue eyes studied her. "You the one who sells the nightgowns?" he asked.

He was looking for the sales clerk who'd sold the nightgown to Senator Ritchie.

He must have heard the newscast about Angie. He didn't know her name or what she looked like, but he'd picked up enough from this morning's TV to bring him here. What thoughts lurked behind those scrutinizing eyes?

Angie couldn't cope with this, she decided. Taking a deep, calming breath, she answered him. "If you tell me what size and color you want, I'll show you what we have."

He continued to stare at her before shaking his head. "Never mind. I've decided not to look at nightgowns today," he said. With that, he turned and strode off.

Liz's pulse was still racing when Angie appeared only a minute later, saying she was sorry she was gone so long.

She didn't look at all distraught, Liz thought. "Quick. Tell me what happened before a customer interrupts," she said. Hearing Angie's account of her talk with the personnel manager would help her get over her chilling encounter with Gerhardt.

"Gloria thinks everything will be all right," Angie replied, with a big smile. "While I was in her office she made some phone calls. She told me to go back to work and she will let me know before I leave tonight what is going to happen. Oh, Liz, thank you for suggesting this."

This Gloria must have clout with Sohms' big shots, Liz decided. "That's great, Angie," she said.

When a customer approached the counter just then, Liz decided to leave. "Call me later and let me know what happens, okay, Angie?"

"Okay," Angie replied.

It had only been a few minutes since Gerhardt took off so abruptly. Liz made sure he was not still waiting for the elevator before she left the floor. If he saw her leaving the store, he might follow her.

Even though everyone at Sohms would eventually put two and two together, it looked as if Angie might not be fired, she thought, as she walked to the subway. But what about Gerhardt? Though she'd covered for Angie this morning, this wasn't the end of it. He would return to the store another day to confront the sales clerk who'd gone to the *Informer* with the nightgown information. He blamed that clerk for giving Nadine the blackmail idea which led to her murder, and he believed *she* was that clerk. When he went back to Sohms, he'd find out Angie was the one.

On the subway, these disturbing thoughts continued to plague her. She had no doubt he was out to get revenge. What did he have in mind? Her concern for Angie heightened. Why hadn't she warned her?

It was unlikely Gerhardt would go back to Sohms today. He thought he'd found the woman who'd started Nadine on her fatal mission and he wanted time to plan his revenge. He'd return to the store in a day or two. When he found out Angie was the woman he blamed, what then? She prayed his revenge wouldn't go beyond harassment and that it would not go on for any length of time.

Then she reminded herself if Gerhardt went back to the store tomorrow, of course the clerk he thought had given Nadine the idea of blackmail would not be there, nor would Angie. She'd warn Angie tomorrow on their way to Grandma's. Then, when he came into the store again, Angie could pretend the sales clerk he'd spoken to had quit. Since he didn't know the clerk's name or where she lived, she and Angie would both be in the clear. She left the subway feeling much better.

WHEN SHE REACHED her building she saw Rosa Moscaretti looking out her front window. They both waved. She wondered if Rosa had seen her leave earlier and was watching to see when she returned. Keeping an eye on her as per Pop's instructions, she thought, as she climbed the stairs to her apartment.

A moment after she was inside, she saw the package containing Mom's birthday present on the table next to the sofa. If she didn't mail it today it might not get to Florida in time. She decided to turn around and go right out with it before she forgot.

She picked up the package and opened the door. Just as she stepped over the threshold, her heart gave a sickening lurch. She found herself face-to-face with Kurt Gerhardt!

Before she could scream, he clapped his hand over her mouth, shoved her back inside and slammed the door shut behind them.

EIGHT

INSIDE THE APARTMENT, he kept his hand over her mouth, pushed her across the room and turned the TV on, full blast. A noisy commercial was in progress.

"Now you can scream all you want," he said, uncovering her mouth.

With her heart racing and her pulses pounding, she tried to think of a way out of this predicament. Not only would her own TV drown out any screaming, but if Joe Moscaretti was watching a Saturday ball game in their living room, directly below, there was no way he or Rosa would hear her.

She cursed herself for her carelessness. She should have made certain Gerhardt had left the store before she went out onto the street. And she should have looked around very carefully before she started walking to the subway. Whether in the store or outside, he'd spotted her, quite by accident because he wouldn't have expected her to leave her job at that hour, and followed her. His bruising grip on her arm told her he still thought she was the clerk responsible for his girlfriend's ill-conceived scheme.

She took a deep breath to keep her voice from trembling. "Suppose you tell me what this is all about," she managed to say.

His face, already hard with anger, grew harder still.

"I know you recognize me from when I was in the store," he said. "Nadine Berkman was my girlfriend. If it hadn't been for you going to her with the dirt about Senator Ritchie, she'd still be alive."

"She'd still be alive if she hadn't decided to use that dirt to blackmail him," Liz replied.

He scowled. "That's not the way I see it. I hold you responsible for her death. I will not let you get away with this."

Her fear should have risen. Instead, it ebbed as her Irish temper flared. "If you're smart you'll get out of here as quick as you can," she said.

She thought he looked uncertain. He glanced around the room. Then he must have figured out it was a one-room apartment because he gave an unpleasant-sounding laugh. "Why? You got a big dog in here? I don't hear any barking. And I don't see any big man either."

He grabbed her purse and went through it. For a moment she breathed a sigh of relief. If all he intended to do was rob her, let him. "Take whatever you find in there and get out," she said.

"I'm not a thief," he said, throwing down her purse. "I just wanted to make sure you didn't have a phone in there."

Pop had wanted her to get a cell phone before he and Mom moved to Florida. They would have given her one if she hadn't convinced them she didn't need it. She glanced at her telephone on the table next to the sofa. One move in that direction and he'd be after her like a storm trooper.

She didn't even want to imagine what he had in mind

for revenge. Her only chance of never finding out lay in her wits. *Think...*

"Well, now that you know I don't have a cell phone, would you mind giving me a little privacy?" she asked. "I need to use the bathroom."

She wasn't surprised when he shot her a suspicious look. Using the bathroom was such a clichéd ploy.

"Where's the bathroom?" he asked.

When she motioned towards the door next to the kitchenette, he nodded. Still gripping her arm, he shoved her towards it. In the bathroom he looked around to make sure it had no means of escape, then started checking it out. She knew he thought she had a cell phone stashed there, somewhere, or maybe some kind of weapon.

He searched through the medicine cabinet. He peered behind the shower curtain into the tub. He looked under the sink, even behind the toilet. Gestapo mentality, she decided, watching him rummage through the laundry hamper and trash can.

At last he turned towards the door. "Okay," he said. "Take your time. We're not going anywhere."

She closed the bathroom door behind him and slid the bolt.

Now she had to find something made of metal— something heavy enough to bang on the floor and make enough noise for the Moscarettis to hear over their TV and her own. She knew they'd come upstairs to find out what all the racket was about.

She glanced around the room. The brass trash can would do. She picked it up and whacked it on the vinyl flooring a few times. It made a terrible noise. She did it again several more times. Ball game or not, Rosa and Joe would hear it.

Gerhardt's voice came through the door. "I'm wise to what you're trying to do. Knock it off or I'll break the door in."

If the banging on the floor didn't bring the Moscarettis to her apartment, the sound of a crashing door certainly would, she thought. She battered the trash can on the floor again, as hard as she could.

This time there was no response from Gerhardt. She pressed her ear to the door. All was silent on the other side. Could he have gone? He must have. He wasn't stupid. He knew all that racket would attract attention.

With a feeling of triumph, she unlocked the door. Cautiously, she ventured out. The apartment appeared to be empty. In this small area there was no place to hide. He'd gone.

Rosa Moscaretti's voice sounded outside the apartment door. "Can you hear me, dearie? Are you all right?" A key rasped in the lock. Seconds later Liz was engulfed in a hug.

"Thank God you're okay," Rosa said. "I knew something was wrong when I heard all that noise. I said to Joe, 'Liz is trying to signal us.' I told him I saw a man come into the building right after you. I thought he was going to Mr. Klein's apartment, I said, but maybe he followed you and broke into your apartment. 'I'm calling the police,' I told Joe."

"I'm thankful you figured out I was sending a distress signal," Liz replied. "The man you saw forced his way in when I opened the door to go out again. When I started pounding on the floor he must have realized someone would hear the noise and come to investigate. Too bad he got away."

"He didn't get away. While I called the police, Joe got his service revolver from when he was in the Marines and caught him running down the stairs. He's holding him in our kitchen till the cops get here."

Just as Rosa spoke, Liz heard footsteps and voices from the hallway below.

"The cops are here," Rosa said. "Come down to our place, dearie. They'll want you to identify the man."

In the Moscaretti's kitchen, two uniforms, one young—probably a rookie—and the other middle-aged, had just arrived. The elder one was conducting a weapons search; the rookie was scrutinizing Gerhardt's ID. Gerhardt looked considerably less like a Nazi storm trooper than he had when he was mouthing off in her apartment, Liz noticed.

"Kurt Gerhardt," the rookie said. "Police interviewed you a couple of nights ago in connection with the Waldorf murders."

Gerhardt bristled. "Yes, I was asked a few questions, but that's all. I'm not a suspect. You should know that."

"You're pretty cocky for someone who just broke into one of my apartments and held one of my tenants against her will," Joe said, still brandishing his gun.

He noticed Liz standing in the doorway with Rosa. "Here's the young lady now, Officers. She'll tell you all about this punk breaking in and how she escaped by locking herself in the bathroom."

The two cops looked at Liz. She knew they were waiting for her statement.

"He didn't actually break in," she said. "He pushed his way in when I opened the door to go out." Not that she intended to minimize Gerhardt's actions, but she wanted to be accurate.

"You're identifying this man as the one who forced his way into your apartment and held you against your will?" the elder officer asked.

"Yes."

"Did he assault you in any way?"

"He grabbed my arm and pushed me."

"Did he threaten you?" Liz hesitated. Gerhardt's statement still sounded in her mind. *"I'm not going to let you get away with this."*

But if she told the cops he'd said that, they'd want to know what she'd done to anger him. She'd have to spill all the details about changing places with Angie. This might lead to Angie's identity being revealed all over the news. It might have an ill effect on her already shaky situation at work.

Before she could decide how to answer, Gerhardt looked directly at her and spoke. "I wasn't going to hurt you. I only wanted to scare you."

"Scare her?" the cops asked, in unison. "Why?"

"She's the salesgirl who sold the nightgown to that murdered senator," he replied. "My girlfriend was the one killed with him at the Waldorf. If it hadn't been for her going to the *Informer* and selling information, my girlfriend would still be alive. Scaring her is little enough for what she did."

"What do you mean, *salesgirl?*" Rosa exclaimed.

"Yeah," Joe added. "She's no salesgirl. She works for the county medical examiner. Tell them, Liz."

The elder cop looked at Liz. "Is that right, ma'am?"

She nodded, "Yes."

Both officers looked puzzled. "Then why did this man think you were a sales clerk?" the rookie asked.

"Who knows?" Rosa replied, before Liz could even open her mouth.

"Yeah," Joe said. "It's clearly a case of mistaken identity. Arrest this punk and get him out of here, officers."

"We'll need you to press charges, ma'am," the elder cop said to Liz.

Pressing charges meant Gerhardt would be arrested.

There'd be court procedures which would surely make the news. Everything about Angie would come out.

She glanced at Gerhardt. He glanced back at her. The menacing aura of the Gestapo agent had disappeared. He looked puzzled, beaten and sad. All her instincts told her she had nothing more to fear from him.

"I don't want to press charges," she said.

Joe cast her an astonished look. "You want this hood back on the streets, Liz?"

"I don't believe he's a threat to me or anyone else," she replied. "Don't forget, his girlfriend was murdered. The shock impaired his judgment."

"If you're sure that's the way you want it, ma'am," the elder officer said. He turned to Gerhardt. "You're free to go, but stay away from this lady, understand?"

Gerhardt looked as if he couldn't believe he'd been

let go. For a moment he stood there staring at Liz. Then he walked towards the door and just before he went out he turned and looked at her again. "Thank you," he said. And then he was gone.

Both Moscarettis told her she should have pressed charges. Joe said he should have done it himself. After all, the punk had invaded his premises. Rosa told her she was too tender-hearted and she hoped Gerhardt wouldn't start stalking her.

"I'm certain I've seen the last of Kurt Gerhardt," Liz told them. Something in his eyes when he thanked her told her he'd given up getting his revenge.

"If he shows up anywhere you're at, report it," the cops told her before they left.

Over the protests of Rosa and Joe, she went out a little while later to mail Mom's birthday present.

"That bum could be waiting around the corner to pounce on you," Rosa said.

But all of Liz's instincts told her that Gerhardt would not bother her again, nor would he go back to Sohms, looking for the sales clerk he blamed for Nadine's death. It was over.

ANGIE PHONED that evening. "Gloria thinks everything is going to be all right," she announced. "I am being transferred to another department, temporarily."

Until the furor about the Waldorf murders subsided, Liz thought. "That's great," she said. "Now, are you all set for my grandmother's tomorrow?"

"Oh, yes," Angie replied. "After what happened today, I am ready for a pleasant time."

Me, too, Liz thought. She decided she wouldn't tell

Angie what happened with Gerhardt. It might upset her and she wouldn't enjoy herself tomorrow. Angie hadn't mentioned hearing about Juan's police interrogation. If she knew he hadn't been arrested, maybe her suspicions about him would end.

While eating microwaved frozen lasagne, Liz flipped through the TV news channels to see if anything new had developed in the Waldorf case. Nothing. Eichle must have found out *something* since Thursday, but whatever it was, he was keeping mum. Since Thursday he'd questioned Gerhardt and Angie and Juan, and she was sure he'd gone back to talk to Mrs. Ritchie again. Then there was the big blonde woman seen on TV with Mrs. Ritchie. Did he suspect she might be Ms. Extra Large?

All this speculation gave her an uncomfortable, restless feeling. This is how addicts must feel, she thought. Her need to find out more about the Waldorf murders was like an alcoholic's craving for a drink or a junkie's for a fix. But she might as well grin and bear it. It looked as if Eichle wasn't going to let her in on anything anymore. Disappointment compounded her restless feeling. He'd been so nice lately. She'd thought it was permanent. She'd even thought they were close to becoming friends.

Well, if he wasn't going to give her any more information, she wouldn't have to tell him about her experience with Gerhardt. He'd hit the ceiling if he knew she'd gotten herself into what could have been real trouble. *Or would he?* The thought of him not being furious with her left her slightly depressed.

She'd just finished washing the dishes when her

doorbell rang. Probably the Moscarettis checking up on her, she thought. Before she got to the door, the bell rang again, and then twice more. Joe and Rosa wouldn't do that. After the first ring, Rosa would call out, "Are you there, dearie?"

She felt a clutch of fear. Gerhardt. *Could her instincts about him have been wrong?*

NINE

SHE KNEW ROSA AND JOE were home. The faint but un-mistakable aroma of pasta sauce wafted up from their kitchen.

Disappointment mingled with her apprehension as she hurried to the phone to call them. She'd been certain Gerhardt had given up his plan for revenge and wouldn't bother her again. How could she have been so wrong? Her instincts had never let her down before.

Just as she picked up the phone, the doorbell sounded again, followed by a familiar voice. "Open up, Rooney— I know you're in there."

Feeling relieved, even a bit pleased, she opened the door. "How did you know I wasn't out, Eichle?" she asked.

"You have a couple of watchdogs downstairs," he said, striding in. "The minute I set foot in the building they were out of their apartment and onto me like a pair of rottweilers." He had on his Detective Sour-Puss face.

"What's your problem?" she asked.

"You," he replied.

"Me? How could I be a problem? I haven't seen or heard from you since the night you took off to question Gerhardt."

"Gerhardt," he growled. "Did you think I wouldn't find out what happened today?"

She should have known he'd get wind of the police report. "It was no big deal. I was planning to tell you if you ever got in touch with me again," she said.

He sank down onto the couch, frowning, shaking his head. "How did you get mixed up with Gerhardt? I want straight answers, Rooney."

"It's not something I can explain in a few words," she replied, sitting down beside him.

He stretched his long legs out and settled back. "Take as much time as you need. I'm off duty."

He listened without interruption while she told him everything in detail. "I was only trying to help Angie—to keep her from being identified as the sales clerk involved," she concluded.

He muttered a mild epithet under his breath. "How do you get yourself in these messes?"

She knew he was reminding her of the last case when she'd put herself at risk in much the same way. "I can't help it if I feel sorry for people," she replied.

"You don't have to befriend every stray dog who comes along," he said.

She bristled. "I resent you referring to Angie like that."

"I was referring to Gerhardt. Why in blazes didn't you have him charged?" Without waiting for a reply, he added, "You're much too trusting, Rooney."

"If you could have seen him…"

"That's exactly what I mean. He put on an act and you fell for it."

"It wasn't an act. His girlfriend…"

"Yeah, I know. He was overcome with grief for a woman he didn't treat so hot when she was alive. The man conned you, Rooney."

There was no use trying to convince him that Gerhardt would not bother her again. "If you came here to heckle me about this, I've heard enough," she said, getting to her feet.

He remained seated. The suggestion of a smile crossed his face. "I was planning to get in touch with you this weekend, anyway. When I heard Gerhardt had forced his way into your apartment, I decided to come right over."

He was telling her he'd planned to let her know more about the Waldorf case. Her annoyance with him dwindled. "So you thought you'd bring me up to date on the murder suspects and bawl me out at the same time," she said.

A grin spread over his face. "I haven't finished bawling you out yet, but I can do that later. I know you want to hear what's been happening the last couple of days. I guess you heard on the news we interviewed Juan Vega."

"Yes, but you didn't arrest him."

"Not enough to go on." He hesitated. "We're not writing him off yet, though. Did your friend Angie tell you about her interview at the station house?"

"She did. Thanks for being so nice to her."

"We're always nice when people cooperate."

Was he going to tell her he'd dropped Angie off at Sohms on his way to question Mrs. Ritchie again, or would she have to drag it out of him?

"She said you drove her to the store so she wouldn't

be late getting to work. That was going out of your way to be kind."

"I was going up Fifth Avenue and had to drive right past there anyway." He cast her a quizzical look. "I get the feeling you already know I went to talk to Mrs. Ritchie again."

"I didn't exactly know, but I thought you might have. Are you going to fill me in?"

"That's one of the reasons I'm here. I know you must have seen the tall blonde with Mrs. Ritchie on TV and you're curious."

"Of course I'm curious. The minute I saw her I thought *Big Bertha*. Who is she and why didn't you tell me about her after your first interview with Mrs. Ritchie instead of waiting for me to see her on TV?"

"She's Mrs. Ritchie's niece. I didn't tell you about her because I didn't know she existed the first time I went there. She must have been out, and Mrs. Ritchie never mentioned her. I guess she was still in shock. Anyway, I didn't see the big blonde until that TV shot." He grinned. "I had the same reaction as you did. I went back to talk with Mrs. Ritchie again as soon as I could, intending to interview the niece, too."

"So you interviewed the big blonde the second time you went there?"

"No. She wasn't there then, either. She'd gone to attend a wedding in Boston. She wanted to cancel because of the senator's death, Mrs. Ritchie said, but the bride was a very close friend and Mrs. Ritchie insisted she go."

"You mean you still haven't seen her?"

"Right. But when I interviewed Mrs. Ritchie the

second time she was feeling better and more talkative. She told me all about her niece. Name's Pamela Enright. She's been living with the Ritchies in Washington for more than a year, serving as Mrs. Ritchie's secretary and companion."

"When are you going to question the niece?"

"Not for a couple of days. Mrs. Ritchie's in Massachusetts now. Her husband's funeral is tomorrow. She said her niece is going to join her and they'll come back to Manhattan on Wednesday. They'll stay with Mrs. Ritchie's friends for a couple of days before heading back to Washington."

Liz had been geared up, ready to hear some good, solid evidence that Mrs. Ritchie's niece was Big Bertha. Now she felt let down. Her disappointment must have shown on her face.

"Smile," he said. "Mrs. Ritchie provided some interesting information. She said her niece took the day off last Tuesday. She left the house that morning and didn't get back till nearly midnight."

Tuesday. The day of the murders. Liz did some quick calculating. This Pamela Enright could have made it to New York, committed the murders, and returned to Washington within the time frame.

"I know what you're thinking," he said.

"It all fits, doesn't it?" she asked.

He shook his head. "None of the airlines show a Pamela Enright on any of the early flights or evening flights either."

"How about the train?"

"That wouldn't work out, time-wise. She could have

made the round trip by car. She doesn't own one but we're still checking auto rentals."

With ID mandatory before boarding flights, she couldn't have used an assumed name, Liz thought. And she'd have to show her driver's license to rent a car. Maybe she borrowed a car.

As if he knew her thoughts, he said, "I inquired about her borrowing a car, but according to Mrs. Ritchie, Pamela had no close friends around Washington. She'd only lived here a year or so."

No close friends that Mrs. Ritchie knew about. She'd give this some more thought and get back to it later, Liz decided. "Does Mrs. Ritchie seem fond of her niece?" she asked.

"I got that impression. According to Mrs. Ritchie, Pamela went through a bitter divorce from a no-good husband who'd gambled away everything her parents left her. She was having a rough time of it. Mrs. Ritchie's previous secretary was retiring, so she offered the job to her niece."

"Do you think Mrs. Ritchie has any suspicions about her niece?"

"If she does, she could win an Oscar."

"So you questioned her without giving your thoughts away? That must have been tricky, even for a skilled interrogator like you."

"What are you up to with your Irish blarney?"

"I want to know what else you talked about the second time you interviewed Mrs. Ritchie."

"Okay. The second time I went to see her she couldn't seem to stop talking about her husband. She told me they were high school sweethearts and how she always knew he was going to make it big someday. Did you know he was a state legislator before he ran for the senate?"

"No. I'd never even heard of him before he became a U.S. senator and started appearing on TV talk shows preaching about morals. And ranting about drug smuggling, and the need for stricter immigration laws. I recall he spoke out for drastic gun control, too, as part of his campaign against corruption and crime."

Eichle nodded. "He wanted to make it illegal for any citizen outside law enforcement and the military to own a gun. No guns, less crime and corruption. I wish it were that easy."

"Did Mrs. Ritchie say anything about his run for the presidential nomination?"

"Not much. I got the feeling she knew he didn't have a chance."

"I wonder why he thought he did."

"She said he was counting on a backlash from voters fed up with what he called the country's declining moral values. He thought of himself as a crusader for decency. She said it was his dream to turn the country around. It's my opinion he had a tremendous ego and he thought his Hollywood good looks would help him."

An egotistical hypocrite, Liz thought. "I don't suppose Mrs. Ritchie said anything about the woman found with him in his hotel suite."

"Surprisingly enough, she did. I don't know if she believes this or not, but she said Nadine must have been there to interview him for her newspaper and the blackmail plan was invented later by the *Informer* to help sell more papers."

"That's delusional. How did she explain the night-gown?"

"She said he bought it for *her*."

"Oh, right. Like he wouldn't know her size after forty years of marriage."

"She also thinks the killer was someone who got into the room intending to rob her husband at gunpoint, and when he and Nadine tried to get the gun away from the robber they were shot in the struggle."

"Well, at least that makes some sense. Did she have any idea why the killer would leave the gun at the scene?"

"She explained it the same as I did when we first talked about this—panic. That's why nothing was taken out of either the senator's wallet or Nadine's."

"Are you going to see Mrs. Ritchie again?"

"Yes. When I interview the niece after they get back from Massachusetts."

By that time he'd know if Pamela had rented a car, Liz thought. The mileage could be checked to find out how far the car had been driven. Another thought struck her: if Pamela and the senator had planned a tryst at the Waldorf, he might have had someone on his staff rent the car and she just picked it up. No doubt Eichle hadn't overlooked this possibility. He'd have to question everyone on the senator's staff.

She gave a deep sigh. "It's going to be tough."

"What's going to be tough?"

"Proving that the niece committed the murders."

"You're way ahead of me, Rooney."

She stared at him, surprised. "Are you saying you don't think she did it?"

"I'm saying it's still too soon for that speculation."

"Why? She's been living under the same roof as the senator for a year, which means they know each other rather well. We both agree the nightgown would be the right size for her. She was gone all day and half the night last Tuesday…"

"If we can't put her in Manhattan the day of the murders we can't make a case."

"Suppose you can't. Could this wind up as an unsolved case?"

"No. Pamela Enright is not the only suspect."

"Who? You've already questioned Gerhardt and Juan Vega and didn't arrest either of them. Are you saying you suspect Mrs. Ritchie, even with her alibi?"

"I didn't say that."

"Pamela's the only one who ties in with the nightgown," she insisted.

Suddenly he frowned. "Speaking of other suspects— I didn't finish bawling you out about your incident with Gerhardt. I want your word that you'll be more careful from now on."

"Sounds like he's still a suspect. I thought he was working late that night and couldn't possibly have followed Nadine to the Waldorf."

"We've crossed Gerhardt off the suspect list but if I had a list of individuals I want you to steer clear of, he'd be at the top."

This was something a friend would say, not someone who was only being nice to her because she'd come up with an important clue in his last case. She covered her surprise with a flippant remark. "Is that so? Who else would be on your list—Juan Vega?"

He cast her a questioning glance. "Why do you think Vega would make my list?"

She'd never been any good at lying. She found herself telling him about her encounter with Juan outside of Radio City Music Hall.

"I shouldn't even have mentioned it," she said. "I'm not even sure he followed me. He could have run into me by chance."

Eichle nodded. "That's probably it. No use getting paranoid over a chance encounter."

His reaction surprised her. She'd expected him to be concerned.

"But didn't you tell me Juan's still a suspect?" she asked. The instant the words were out she wished she could take them back. Now he'd think she wanted him to be concerned about her.

She felt relieved when he seemed not to have heard her question. Instead, he asked one of his own. "If you haven't eaten yet, how about going out for a pizza and a beer?"

Of course she'd eaten. She wasn't any good at lying, but… "Pizza and a beer would be great," she replied.

She knew they'd reached a temporary impasse as far as the Waldorf murders were concerned, but she sensed their potential for friendship was off and running.

TEN

GOING OUT FOR PIZZA with Eichle had been the closest thing to a date she'd had since she'd dumped Wade, Liz thought as she drank her coffee the following morning. Their dinner Thursday night didn't count. That was strictly Waldorf murders business. This was more social. They only talked about the case for a few seconds. She'd mentioned the gun found at the scene.

"You haven't said anything about murder weapon lately," she'd said.

"Nothing much to tell. We're still working on it."

"Were the serial numbers filed off?"

"Partially."

"Will you be able to trace it?"

"We're making progress." He looked at her over his beer glass. "Shall we give it a rest, Rooney? The case, I mean."

She was surprised he wanted to talk about something else. Well, she wouldn't mind asking him a few questions about himself. She knew little about his private life. He'd told her once he lived in an apartment near the Battery. She'd heard Pop mention he wasn't married. Surprising. He could be a nice guy when he wasn't being the grouchy detective.

"Sure—let's change the subject," she said. "You can start by telling me about yourself. Where you were born and grew up. Where you went to school. All that stuff."

"I wouldn't want to put you to sleep," he replied.

"How can we carry on a conversation with nothing to go on?"

"We could talk about you."

"I'm sure Pop told you more than you wanted to know about me."

"I wouldn't say that, but you're right, he did tell me a lot. Okay, I'll start the ball rolling. I was born in up-state New York, near Syracuse. Grew up there. Went to school there, including college."

He told her he'd wanted to be a detective ever since he was a kid. "I think it was all those cop and private eye shows on TV during the late eighties and early nineties," he said. "Anyway, I never got over it. My folks knew. They encouraged me to take pre-Law in college, thinking if I became a lawyer my youthful ambition would be satisfied."

"Obviously it wasn't."

"Right. I didn't apply to law school. Instead I came to Manhattan and applied for the NYPD Police Academy. This was about seven years ago."

She did some rough calculations with the years he'd mentioned. He was probably six years older than her. She cast a furtive glance at him. When he wasn't grouchy he could pass for good-looking.

"How about girlfriends?" she asked.

"At present—zero."

That sounded as if he'd recently broken off with someone, she decided.

He cast her a keen glance. "I know what you're thinking. Yes, there was someone a few months ago. She wanted me to quit the force and take a job in her father's investment banking firm."

Liz couldn't imagine him as anything but a homicide detective. "You'd have been bored stiff," she said.

He nodded. "I know."

"Any regrets?"

"Not anymore."

"And you're not seeing anyone at present?"

"Would I have asked you out for pizza and beer if I had a new girlfriend?"

He must have known when he came charging into her apartment on a Saturday night that there was no special person in her life, either, she thought. How could he know this? Pop had moved to Florida before her breakup with Wade. Maybe Eichle and Pop had been in touch and Pop mentioned it to him. However he knew, the circumstances had put them in the same boat. Misery loves company. Except she didn't feel at all miserable without Wade. Eichle didn't seem heartbroken, either.

"I'm glad we're both temporarily on the loose," she said. "It gives us a chance to be friends."

"You're sure you want to be friends with an old curmudgeon like me?"

Old curmudgeon. That sounded as if he knew she and Sophie often referred to him as Detective Pickle-Puss. But of course he couldn't know about that. Anyway, the name didn't seem as fitting anymore.

"Sure I'm sure," she replied.

When the evening ended she felt as if they'd progressed. Maybe it wasn't real friendship yet, but it went well beyond whatever it was they had before.

Now, as she got ready to meet Angie in the St. George ferry terminal, she realized she hadn't given much thought to the murders since Eichle suggested they talk about something else. She turned to a news channel just in time to hear a newscaster report the identity of the blonde woman seen with Mrs. Ritchie on TV a few days ago. The same clip of the two women coming out of the building was shown. No mention was made that police planned to interview niece Pamela Enright when she returned to Manhattan from the senator's funeral. No hint that she might be a possible suspect. If the media managed to shoot more pictures of Pamela, it wouldn't be long before they'd be speculating about her size and making a connection.

The day was mild. On the ferry, she sat on the outside deck. She thought about Pamela Enright. By the time the boat docked, she was more certain than ever that Pamela was Ms. Extra Large and the senator had purchased the nightgown for her. But that didn't necessarily mean Pamela had committed the murders. If it turned out that she hadn't been in Manhattan the day of the murders, then maybe the senator intended to give her the nightgown when he returned to Washington. If so, someone else had shot him and Nadine.

Angie was waiting near the train platform. She looked very chic in a long gray dress with a matching jacket. Unmistakably Sohms Fifth Avenue. No doubt she got a generous employee's discount.

"Am I dressed right?" Angie asked, eyeing Liz's camel color slacks and sweater. "This is what I wear to mass and I came to the ferry directly from church."

She smiled. "Besides, I wanted to look nice for your grandmother."

"You look great," Liz replied. "If I had an outfit like that I'd have worn it."

She noticed more than one passing male giving Angie a second glance. How had Angie escaped an amorous involvement? But of course she hadn't. Liz was almost sure Angie had been romantically involved with Juan before she got it into her head that he had something to do with the Waldorf murders. Angie must have heard on the news that Juan had not been arrested after his questioning. Maybe now she'd have a change of heart.

"I guess you heard the police let Juan go," she said.

Angie nodded. "I was pleased he was not arrested."

"Have you decided he was not involved in the murders?"

"I—I am not sure," Angie said. "I cannot forget how he left the coffeehouse so suddenly after I told him Senator Ritchie was staying at the Waldorf. Where did he go in such a hurry?"

"He must have told the police where he went and the police must have been satisfied, otherwise they'd have arrested him."

The train pulled into the station at that moment. They boarded. When the train cleared the terminal, Angie started a steady stream of chatter.

"Maybe when Mama and Hermano come to the States I will get a house out here," Angie said excitedly.

If she hadn't been fired from her job. Angie hadn't mentioned the final outcome, but she didn't seem worried.

"How did it all turn out at work?"

"Oh, didn't I tell you? Gloria said everything was going to be all right."

"You told me she *thought* everything would be all right and that you were being transferred to another department for a while."

"Yes. I have been working in Children's Clothing all week. Gloria says I can go back to Lingerie when reporters stop coming in and asking questions about me."

"Won't the sales clerks in Lingerie tip off the reporters where to find you?"

"No. They have been told not to answer any questions."

The *Informer* would pay interesting money for some answers, Liz thought.

As if she knew Liz had this thought, Angie dispelled the idea with a strong statement. "Sohms is an excellent place to work. All the employees know there are not many companies who offer such good pay and benefits and especially a chance to get ahead. Look at me, for example."

So, rather than risk losing their jobs for whatever they might be offered, Angie's coworkers would keep mum. "Then I guess you're absolutely certain your job is secure," Liz said.

"Yes, I am."

"Didn't you have to appear before the board of directors or something?"

"Yes. The store manager and two others. Gloria went with me. I was— I forget the word, but it is like being scolded."

"Reprimanded?"

"Yes, that is it. And I was put on six months probation."

"You were lucky you weren't fired."

"I know. Gloria said the store wanted to avoid publicity."

There would have been plenty of that, Liz thought, and all of it bad. When word got out that Sohms had fired someone named Angelita Diaz, every Hispanic organization in the city would be up in arms. She pictured headlines in all the newspapers depicting Angie as a victim of anti-Latino prejudice and discrimination. Never mind what she'd done. The fact that she was young and pretty would add fuel to the journalistic conflagration. Chanting crowds would march around in front of the store with enlarged photos of Angie borne aloft. The demonstrators would increase in numbers with each passing day. Sohms Fifth Avenue would lose business.

Angie's voice penetrated her thoughts. "I think Hermano would like living here more than St. George," she said, watching the landscape flash by. "And Mama could have a flower garden."

By the time the train pulled into the New Dorp station, it seemed to Liz that Angie was much more upbeat about the prospects of bringing her mother and brother to the States. This thought was reinforced when, on the short walk to Gram's house, they passed the parochial school Liz had attended. When Liz pointed it out, Angie said, "Maybe this could be Hermano's school."

Did Angie think Senator Ritchie's death had bettered the chances of bringing her family here? She wanted to tell Angie the death of a bill's sponsor would not change the legislation. But they'd almost reached Gram's house. Liz saw Gram standing on the front porch, waiting for them.

"Is that your grandmother?" Angie asked. "She does not look like the grandmothers in Colombia. There, they would not wear a pantsuit and they would have gray hair—not red like yours."

Liz smiled. As long as Gram could make it to the Crowning Glory Beauty Salon, her hair would always be the russet color she'd passed along to Liz.

Gram greeted them both with a hug and led them into her kitchen where the table was set with the blue and white dishes so familiar to Liz. Being in Gram's kitchen was like taking a step back in time. For a few seconds Liz was a child again, having milk and cookies with Gram after school, waiting for Mom to get there from her schoolteacher job in Port Richmond. The cookie jar, shaped like a cat, still stood on the shelf over the stove.

"Liz said you're from South America, Angie," Gram said, pouring tea from the familiar old teapot. "How do you like living in the United States?"

"I like it so much I intend to become a citizen as soon as I am eligible," Angie replied.

Gram nodded approval. "Did your family come here with you?"

Angie's face grew grave. "No—my mother and brother are still in Colombia. I have been trying for a long time to bring them here, but…" Her voice trailed off.

"I'll bet I know what happened," Gram said. "It was Senator Ritchie's immigration bill, wasn't it?"

"Yes," Angie replied. Her face brightened. "But now that he is dead maybe things will change."

Liz shot Gram a warning glance and spoke the first thought that came into her head. "Angie's mother is not well and Angie is very anxious to have her come here," she said. She didn't want Gram to tell Angie that the senator's death would not change the legislation. Angie would find this out, soon enough. Why spoil her day?

Gram got the message. "Oh. I'm sorry to hear that," she said placing a green salad and tuna fish sandwiches on the table. She shook her head. "It beats me how that immigration bill ever got passed, and for that matter how Senator Ritchie ever got to Washington."

"Those Massachusetts voters must have been dazzled by his good looks," Liz said.

"That's exactly what happened," Gram said. "You remember Mrs. Dooley over on Third Street, don't you, Liz? Well, she comes from the same town as Senator Ritchie and his wife. Some place near Boston. Went to the same high school and knew them both. They were high school sweethearts, she says."

Liz's senses went on alert. "You never told me this before, Gram."

"Didn't know about it myself till the murders," Gram said. "Mrs. Dooley dug out her high school yearbook when she heard. She showed me their pictures. Jason Ritchic was very good-looking and Ellen Barber—that was Mrs. Ritchie's maiden name—she was like a little blonde doll."

"This is very interesting," Liz said. "Do you think Mrs. Dooley would let me look at the yearbook?"

Gram looked dubious. "I don't know, dear. Once the

word got out she knew the Ritchies and had the year-book the whole neighborhood's been asking to see it."

"Could you give her a call, Gram, and find out if there's any chance I could look at it today?"

"I know you're following the case, but it's not likely anything in the yearbook would shed light on the murders," Gram said.

"I just want to find out what kind of boy Senator Ritchie was. Please, Gram."

Gram took a sip of her tea. "It wouldn't hurt to try. I'll call Mrs. Dooley now."

"What is this book?" Angie asked.

While Liz explained, Gram went to the telephone. She came back a few minutes later saying that Mrs. Dooley would drop by a little later with the yearbook.

With a sense of excitement, Liz waited. She wasn't sure what she expected to find in the yearbook. Some hint of the traits that shaped the character of Jason Ritchie, perhaps, or some foreshadowing of what the future held.

Mrs. Dooley, a large, florid woman somewhere in her 50s, arrived.

Gram introduced them. "Sheila, you remember my granddaughter Liz Rooney, and this is her friend, Angie."

"Thanks for allowing us to look at your yearbook, Mrs. Dooley," Liz said. "I'm very interested in seeing it."

"Isn't everybody?" Mrs. Dooley said. "I don't dare let it out of my sight."

It was plain the yearbook had given Mrs. Dooley celebrity status in the neighborhood. She handed the book to Liz, then sat down nearby. She meant what she said about not letting it out of her sight.

Liz turned at once to the class photographs. "Here he is," she said. "Jason Paul Ritchie…" His face was recognizable, even though his dark hair would later turn the silvery gray so familiar to TV viewers.

"He was very handsome," Angie said. "And look at all the things he did in school."

Liz went down the list, commenting to Angie about each achievement.

"President, Senior Class; President, Student Council. A vote-getter, even then."

"Debating Team. Was good at making speeches too."

"Drama Club, Senior Play. He brought his dramatic flair into politics."

"Track Team, Swim Team. Enough of an athlete to round him out."

"Rifle Club, Rifle Team. Wait a minute! What about his stand against guns?"

She wanted to linger over Jason Ritchie's picture and record, to give this about-face on guns some more thought, but even though Mrs. Dooley was engrossed in conversation with Gram, she felt a bit hurried. She looked up Mrs. Ritchie's picture.

Ellen Louise Barber. Blonde. Pretty.

Honor Roll, Honor Society, Library Volunteer, Literary Society, Art Club, School Choir…

Ellen had been a serious student, quite the opposite of Jason. Somehow they'd stuck together. The quiet little wife had faded into the background while her flamboyant husband went on to become a political combination of Billy Graham and Paul Newman.

Flipping the pages, Liz came to the class predictions. "Look here, Angie," she said, "it says Jason Ritchie would become a big Hollywood star, a TV evangelist or President of the United States. Is that an accurate prophecy or what?"

"It is as if he had not changed at all since high school," Angie replied.

Liz nodded. "My thoughts, exactly." She flipped through some more pages, looking for a picture of the Rifle Team. There he was, Jason Ritchie with several other boys standing with their coach, holding their rifles, barrels down. There was no mistaking the proud looks on their faces. These guys loved their guns.

Angie looked surprised. "He has changed his mind about guns. Now he would not want anybody except police and soldiers to have them."

Mrs. Dooley overheard. "I don't believe for one minute he changed," she said with a sniff. "Everyone in school knew Jason Ritchie was crazy about guns. My cousin was on the Rifle Team and he told me Jason had a gun collection. Probably still has, only bigger. It's like him and Ellen. He was crazy about her, too. All through high school he never looked at another girl. You can't tell me he'd ever cheat on her."

"So why was Nadine Berkman in his hotel room?" Gram asked.

"To interview him for her newspaper. Sure, it's a scandal sheet, but sometimes they print interviews with decent people. Like I said, he was a one-woman man."

"But the nightgown…"

"According to the news it was too big for that reporter anyway. He bought it for some woman relative—maybe that tall blonde on TV. I heard on the news she's Ellen's niece. Pamela, her name is. Ellen probably told him, 'While you're in New York, get something for Pamela's birthday.' The police should have found out if any of his women relatives had birthdays coming up."

It had been about forty years since Jason Ritchie and Ellen Barber were high school sweethearts. The senator could have developed a roving eye since then, Liz thought, but she wasn't going to argue this point with Mrs. Dooley.

"Besides being a one-girl guy, what sort of boy was he?" she asked.

"He was kind of stuck-up," Mrs. Dooley replied. "He knew he was handsome. He was voted best-looking boy in the class."

"Stuck—up—like conceited?"

"Yes."

"So you didn't like him?"

"I didn't dislike him. He was all right. He was always nice to everyone."

A politician even then, Liz thought. Also an actor and an orator.

"When he made speeches, were they anything like the ones he made after he became a senator?" she asked.

"If you mean did he speak about morals and the country going down the tubes, sure he did. The kids used to say in some of his debates he sounded like a preacher."

So the Saintly Senator was working on his halo even in high school. Liz found herself agreeing with Mrs. Dooley. He was a man whose values and habits would not have changed over the years. This one-squaw brave would not have strayed off the reservation. Nor would the gun-crazy member of the Rifle Team have stopped collecting. His collection would be extensive by now, but kept under wraps because of his stand against civilian gun ownership.

A startling possibility struck her. Suppose the murder weapon was a gun from Senator Ritchie's collection!

Would the senator have taken one of his guns on a flight to New York? Common sense ruled this out. Airport security would have discovered it. Besides, what possible reason would there have been for him to do that?

Mrs. Dooley slid to the edge of her chair. "Are you almost done looking? I don't want to rush you, but there's others wanting to see it this afternoon."

Liz took a final glance at the picture of teenaged Jason Ritchie with his gun. "Yes. I'm finished," she said. "Thanks, Mrs. Dooley."

She'd learned something from the yearbook, she thought, something almost indisputable. Jason Ritchie had held on to the values and attachments of his youth. She'd branded him a hypocrite for his womanizing. Now she wondered if his hypocrisy lay solely in his present stand on gun control.

"Well, how about that?" Gram said, closing the front door behind Mrs. Dooley. "Here I've been thinking the senator was into hanky-panky with that nightgown. Now I'm not so sure."

"I'm not sure about that anymore either," Liz said.

Angie nodded. "Nor I."

"I'm surprised the homicide detectives didn't check out what kind of boy the senator was," Gram said. "If your father was on the case, he'd have done that, first thing, Liz."

Had Eichle made any attempt at this? Liz wondered. Probably not. It was a wispy idea, but she'd certainly tell him what she'd found out today anyway. Whenever he showed up on her doorstep again.

"If it wasn't a woman coming in and finding the senator with that reporter, then it must have been someone with a grudge," Gram went on. "Like the reporter's jealous boyfriend or that Puerto Rican terrorist."

"Police questioned both of them and didn't arrest either," Liz said, glancing at Angie. "And the Puerto Rican man isn't a terrorist, Gram, he's a Nationalist."

"Same thing," Gram said, with a shrug. "I remember when Puerto Ricans tried to assassinate President Truman."

"There is something I should tell you, Mrs. McGowan," Angie said. "This Puerto Rican man, he is a friend of mine."

Gram looked startled. "Oh. I'm sorry, dear. I shouldn't have spoken out like that when I don't even know the man. I hope you'll forgive me, Angie."

Angie's eyes misted. "There is nothing to forgive. I, too, have suspected Juan had something to do with the murders."

"Is this Juan more than just a friend?" Gram asked.

"I was beginning to think that way," Angie replied.

"But now I do not know what to think and I am not sure how I feel."

"Angie, if Juan had any connection to the murders, Eichle would have arrested him," Liz said.

Gram looked interested. "Isn't Eichle that young cop your father likes so much?"

"Yes. He's on the Waldorf case with another detective."

Gram's eyes brightened. "Have you been seeing him?"

"Not really—I mean—well, we get together once in a while to talk about the case."

She held back a sigh. Within a scant minute, Gram had decided that Angie was in love with Juan and gotten the notion that something was developing with Eichle.

"Seems like you girls are up to your necks in this case," Gram said.

She patted Angie's hand. "Liz is right, dear. If your boyfriend had anything to do with the murders, Liz's detective would have arrested him."

Before time came to leave, Angie opened up to Gram even more. In response to gentle questioning, the entire story of her life was confided.

"I feel as if you are my own grandmother," she said, as they hugged goodbye.

"Then you must call me Gram, like Liz does."

"I know what I will call you," Angie replied. *"Abuela."*

"I remember that word from my high school Spanish," Gram said. "Liz's grandmother will be your *abuela*."

When Liz and Angie parted in the ferry terminal,

Angie said she had not enjoyed herself as much since coming to the States.

"I have almost stopped worrying that Juan is involved in the murders," she said. "There is only one thing troubling me. I still feel great guilt about going to that newspaper with the information about Senator Ritchie. I still feel as if the murders were my fault."

"Look at it this way," Liz said. "If the murders hadn't happened, you and I would never have met. There's an old saying—'it's an ill wind that blows no good.'"

Angie nodded. "I understand. There can be some good even in bad situations. My ill wind is the murders and the good is our friendship."

"Keep that in mind for whenever you start feeling guilty," Liz said.

ELEVEN

ON SUNDAY NIGHTS Liz always got a phone call from her parents. She'd been home about an hour when the call came through.

"I guess you've been having fun with the Waldorf case, haven't you, Lizzie?" Pop asked.

She sighed. "Oh, Pop—I wish you were here. Eichle's being letting me in on a few things, but there's a lot he doesn't tell me."

Pop laughed. "I didn't tell you everything when I was on the force, either. So, you and Eichle are getting along better these days?"

"Well, you know I helped him with his last case."

Mom came on the extension. "Maybe that's not the only reason he's easier to get along with."

First Gram, now her parents. Liz wondered how Eichle would react if he knew he was the subject of such speculation. Most likely he'd crawl back into his Detective Sour-Puss shell.

"I went to see Gram today," she said, changing the subject. She told them about Mrs. Dooley's yearbook. "It was really weird. I got the distinct impression that Senator Ritchie hadn't changed since he was in high school. Everything he was interested in back then he was still interested in until the day he died. He even married the girl he dated all through high school. Mrs. Dooley said he never looked at another girl."

"Well, that's one area where he changed," Mom said, her voice dripping with sarcasm.

"Mrs. Dooley doesn't believe Jason Ritchie would cheat on his wife," Liz said.

"Sounds like you're convinced of that too, Lizzie," Pop replied.

"I guess I am. But there's more to this. The senator was on the Rifle Team and Mrs. Dooley said everyone in the school knew he was crazy about guns; her cousin was on the same team and told her Jason collected guns. Mrs. Dooley doesn't believe he could change so drastically about something he was so interested in. She believes he still has his gun collection, only now it's bigger and better."

"If that's true it would be the best kept secret since the atomic bomb," Pop said. "Years ago, when Senator Ritchie ran for the state legislature in Massachusetts, he came out for gun control in a big way. Made it the biggest issue of his campaign. His political opponents dug around and found out he'd been crazy about guns since high school and had started collecting them. They used it against him in the campaign, but the senator got on TV and swore he was now firmly against civilians owning guns and he'd disposed of his gun collection. He won in a landslide."

"How come he made gun control such an issue?"

"Politics. Many voters were antigun at the time. President Reagan had just been shot by a civilian."

"So, this turnabout was just to get elected. Do you

think he lied when he said he'd disposed of his gun collection?"

"Maybe. But if he still continued collecting guns after his political career got going, you can bet your bottom dollar he only dealt with shady characters so there'd be no paper trail, and he kept the guns well hidden. Collectors like to keep their treasures where they can look at them often. That means they'd be stashed somewhere in his Washington house. If anyone knew about his collection it would be his wife. She'd have been the only person who knew he still had the guns and where they were hidden."

Something in his voice alerted Liz. "Pop! Are you saying the murder weapon could be from his collection and that Mrs. Ritchie could have…?" Her voice trailed off. "But she has an airtight alibi."

"Even airtight alibis have been known to puncture," Pop replied.

He'd been teasing her, she thought, after they said goodbye. But the idea settled in her mind.

Next time Eichle dropped in, should she tell him about the yearbook and Senator Ritchie's time warp and run the gun collection idea past him? She knew what his reaction would be. "You're right back where you started, Rooney," he'd say.

But she wasn't. Not exactly. Though it might seem as if Mrs. Ritchie again topped her suspect list, there was another possibility. Pamela Enright had been living in the Ritchies' house for more than a year. What if, contrary to Mrs. Dooley's firm convictions, she and the senator had struck up more than a niece-and-uncle relationship? What if she had, somehow, discovered the cache of guns? What if it turned out she'd been in Manhattan the day of the murders?

But one thing didn't fit. If she and the senator had arranged a rendezvous at the Waldorf, why would she have sneaked a gun out of the collection and taken it to New York with her? She certainly would not have anticipated finding him with another woman and planned the shooting.

With a sigh, Liz realized Eichle's imagined comment would have been right on the mark. She was back where she started with Mrs. Ritchie as her prime suspect.

She turned all this over in her mind while eating a cheeseburger and salad for dinner. After eating she watched TV to see if there was anything new about the murders. There wasn't. At least nothing the police had released to the media.

Her doorbell rang. As she went to the door she found herself hoping she'd see Eichle through the peephole. Now that she'd thought it all over, she wanted to tell him about Senator Ritchie being crazy about guns.

It was Eichle.

"I phoned you a couple of times," he said, easing his rangy form onto the sofa. "The first time there was no answer. Next time I got a busy signal. That meant you were home so I decided to come over."

"I was talking to my folks for a while."

"How are they doing? They still like it in Florida?"

"They're both fine and still love it down there. I told Pop you've been letting me in on some angles about the Waldorf case."

"I have another angle for you. But first some good news. Kurt Gerhardt is leaving town."

"He is? How come?"

"He'd been told to keep us informed of his where-abouts in case we needed to talk to him again. He showed up at the station house today and said he wanted to take a job transfer. There's an immediate opening in the Buffalo branch of his company, he said."

Liz felt a pang of empathy. Gerhardt wanted to distance himself from the scene of his girlfriend's murder. "So you gave him the okay."

"Right. He'll be leaving soon. I thought you'd like to know you won't have to worry about him bothering you anymore."

She wanted to tell him she hadn't been worried, but he seemed pleased with this turn of events. She didn't want to spoil it for him. It was as if he'd cast her in the role of damsel in distress.

His concern touched her. He'd come a long way from *"What are you doing here, Rooney?"* and *"When are you going to quit meddling in police matters?"*

She'd tell him about the information in the yearbook later, she decided. First, she wanted to hear what else he had to tell her. "What's the new angle you have for me?" she asked. She was unprepared for the impact of his reply.

"We now have reason to believe Pamela Enright was in Manhattan the day of the murders."

She was almost too stunned to reply. "How did you find out?"

"Two tips. One placed Pamela in the Oak Room of the Plaza Hotel at lunchtime last Tuesday. The other informant claimed he saw her in an uptown parking garage at 8:00 p.m. Both callers said they recognized her from seeing her on TV and both said they thought she fit the description of the tall woman the police wanted to question."

"How do you know these weren't crank calls? You must have gotten a lot of those."

"We did. We checked them all. These were different."

"Well, how come they didn't phone in right away? It's been nearly a week since the murders."

"Don't forget, we didn't know Pamela's identity right away. The informants phoned in right after she was identified on the news. One of them is a waiter at the Plaza. He said he was sure he'd served Pamela that day. She was having lunch with a man and another couple, he said. He remembered her because she said she was a vegetarian and asked him if the salad she ordered could be served without bacon. He said she was very pleasant and thanked him for his attention to her request, and the man she was with paid the check and left him a generous tip. When he saw her on TV with Mrs. Ritchie he recognized her, but he didn't put it all together till later when he heard on the news she's Mrs. Ritchie's niece."

"Sounds for real. What about the parking garage tip?"

"He said he was on duty at eight last Tuesday night when 'the Ritchie niece'—as he put it—came in with a man. They picked up a black Lexus with Maryland plates."

"He gave you the license number and you traced it."

"Right."

"I don't suppose you're going to tell me who owns the car."

"Right, again. Not yet."

Well, at least she could figure out for herself that, whoever he was, he'd driven Pamela to Manhattan early Tuesday morning, and they'd spent the day there. Also, this male companion owned an expensive car and left big tips. Why hadn't Mrs. Ritchie told Eichle about this man instead of saying Pamela didn't have any close friends around Washington? Answer—Mrs. Ritchie didn't know about him. Pamela hadn't told her. She didn't want her aunt to know she'd been seeing this guy. Why?

"I guess the owner of the Lexus has been questioned," she said, hoping he'd let slip some hint of the car owner's identity.

No such luck. "Yes, and I'm questioning Pamela when she and Mrs. Ritchie get back to Manhattan on Wednesday," he replied.

"What do you make of it, Eichle?"

"Let's just say your guess is as good as mine."

She held back a sigh. He seemed to think if he fed her scraps of information, she'd be satisfied. Instead it only whetted her appetite.

Since he wasn't going to give her any more information, now would be a good time to tell him what she'd picked up from the yearbook. The gun collection idea, especially, might interest him.

"Here's something for you to think about," she said.

He listened without interruption. "I get the feeling you think the possibility of a gun collection figures in the case," he said when she finished.

"Don't you think it might?"

"It's possible, of course. The murder weapon could have been part of the senator's collection, if such a collection exists."

"But you don't think it's probable."

"I didn't say that. It's an interesting idea with interesting implications. I'll give it some thought."

It was clear he wasn't going to discuss the matter further, Liz thought. But at least he hadn't laughed at her suspicions.

"I've got to leave," he said, getting to his feet. "I just wanted to fill you in on Pamela. It won't hit the media for a day or so."

"Thanks. You know how I like being ahead of the media. Will you let me know how it goes with Pamela's questioning?"

"No promises."

At the door, he paused. "Thanks for telling me about the yearbook."

He wouldn't have mentioned the yearbook again if he'd completely shrugged off the gun collection idea, she thought, as she closed the door behind him. She'd given him the idea of the gun collection. If anything came of it, he might feel obligated to tell her how the questioning went.

Mrs. Ritchie and Pamela would be back in Manhattan

on Wednesday, Eichle had said. Most likely she'd hear from him by Thursday. Three days of impatient speculation. But whatever he told her would be worth the wait.

TWELVE

MONDAY'S NEWSPAPERS picked up yesterday's TV item about Pamela's identity. Though the articles were not given front page space in any, Liz was not surprised that the *Daily News* hinted at her physical resemblance to the woman sought for questioning by the police. Soon it would be all over the media that Pamela had been in Manhattan the day of the murders.

She could visualize the kind of headlines in the tabloids—something like:

NIECE'S NIGHTIE OR NOT?

On Tuesday morning she wakened with one thought in mind. One week ago Senator Jason Ritchie and Nadine Berkman were slain at the Waldorf and the police seemed no closer to a solution now than then.

Only one week and already TV newscasters had taken up other events as their lead items and newspapers had started relegating the Waldorf story to inside pages. An embezzlement scandal involving a prominent city office holder now occupied the headlines. Only the *Informer* would still feature the Waldorf case on its front page and then only until something more lurid was uncovered.

It would take a witness stating that he or she had seen

Pamela Enright in the lobby of the Waldorf on Tuesday evening to land the case back in the headlines.

On Wednesday, during the morning, Liz turned on her office TV hoping to catch a news report.

"Just in," a newscaster was saying. "Mrs. Jason Ritchie, widow of the murdered senator, and her niece, Miss Pamela Enright, arrived back in New York this morning after attending the senator's funeral in Massachusetts." A picture came on of Mrs. Ritchie and Pamela getting off a plane at LaGuardia Airport, before the newscaster went on to other items.

The photo shot had been fleeting, but there'd been enough of it to establish Pamela as anything but petite. She towered above her aunt, and Liz was sure if she were walking in front of her instead of beside her, Mrs. Ritchie could not have been seen at all, even though she was wearing her wide-brimmed hat.

The media's reaction to Pamela's size would be interesting.

TODAY WAS MOM'S BIRTHDAY. That evening Liz phoned her.

"The slip came yesterday," Mom said. "Thank you so much, dear. It's beautiful and I love it—but *Sohms*—I know it was terribly expensive."

No need to tell Mom she wouldn't have gone to Sohms if she hadn't wanted to find the sales clerk who sold Senator Ritchie the nightgown. She probably would have bought a slip at Macy's and saved a few bucks. But, despite the protests, she could tell Mom was pleased. That was all that mattered.

She talked to Mom for a while. Then Pop came on.

"I saw Mrs. Ritchie's niece on TV this morning," he said. "Guess I don't have to tell you what I was thinking."

"Probably the same thing I've been thinking," she replied. "If the police want to find Big Bertha they should start with Pamela."

"Big Bertha?"

"That's what Eichle named the woman the nightgown was bought for."

"Sounds like something he'd think up. Good sense of humor. Say hello to him for me when you see him, Lizzie."

"I'll do that."

Eichle would probably interview Pamela today. Maybe she'd hear from him tomorrow.

But Thursday passed with no word from Eichle. He must have questioned Pamela by now, and maybe Mrs. Ritchie, too. She felt annoyed with herself for depending on him for information, but with Sophie gone from the homicide department and Dan still on vacation, he was her only source. Sure, he hadn't made any promises, but he'd been so forthcoming lately…she decided to give him the benefit of the doubt. Maybe he hadn't seen Pamela and Mrs. Ritchie yet. Maybe today was the day and she'd hear from him tomorrow.

Friday. No calls at the office all day. She was fed up with waiting for Eichle to get in touch with her. If he didn't phone or drop in tonight, that probably meant he'd come to her apartment unannounced on Saturday or Sunday night, like he did before.

Did he think she had nothing to do on weekends except sit around and wait for him to appear?

It was almost quitting time when Sophie phoned. "Ralph's tied up tonight and I'm off," she said. "Can you meet me for dinner and take in a movie afterwards?"

"Sure. Where do you want to eat?"

"How about that seafood place on Union Square where we ate a month or so ago? I know it's pricey, but I'm hungry for their crab cakes."

"Crab cakes sound good to me, too. See you there around six?"

"Okay, but don't hang up yet. Ralph asked me to run something by you."

"Can't it wait till we're in the restaurant?"

"It could, but I can't. Are you free Saturday night?"

"Free as a bird. What's up?"

"You remember Ralph telling us about his cousin Phil from Philadelphia?"

"The handsome bachelor? Sure."

"Well—he's in town on business."

"Is this a blind date thing?"

"Yes. Ralph says he's a nice guy. Full of fun, besides being very good-looking. He's sure you two would hit it off. How about it?"

"You're asking someone who hasn't had a real date in nearly a month if she'd like to go out with a handsome, fun-loving bachelor?"

"Is that a yes?"

"With a capital Y."

"Great! We'll pick you up at your place tomorrow night around six. Ralph said Phil's making reservations at the Rainbow Room. We'll talk some more about it while we're having dinner."

The Rainbow Room meant something other than

casual dress. Good thing she'd bought a couple of neat outfits while she was seeing Wade. Should she wear the green silk suit with the long, side-slit skirt, or the black pantsuit with the tunic top and wide legs?

It felt good to be thinking about something other than Eichle's silence.

Angie phoned before she left to meet Sophie. From the moment she heard her voice, Liz could tell she was not in the best of spirits.

"What's wrong?" she asked, hoping Sohms had not reversed its decision to keep Angie on.

"I had another appointment at Immigration," Angie replied. "There has been no progress made about bringing Mama and Hermano into the States."

"Oh, Angie, I'm so sorry. Did they offer any hope?"

"They only said what they always say. It will take time."

Angie needed cheering up. Liz was struck with an idea. "How about spending Sunday with me? Can you ride a bicycle?"

"I have not ridden one in years, but I know how."

"We could go to Central Park and rent bikes and have a picnic."

"Oh, Liz—could we do that?"

"Why not? The weather's been beautiful and the forecast says more of the same."

"Oh," Angie said. "I just remembered I do not have anything I could wear on a bicycle. I will have to buy something."

Angie shouldn't spend money on clothing she wouldn't wear frequently, Liz thought. "I'll lend you some biking pants," she replied.

Angie laughed. "Thank you, but I know I could not squeeze into anything of yours. I am a size ten and you look at least two sizes smaller."

"No problem, I'll ask Sophie to lend you something of hers. She's a ten too."

"You always know what to do about things," Angie said.

"Not always," Liz replied. She wished she knew what to do about Eichle. Should she go on thinking that they were becoming good friends, only to have her feelings dashed when he didn't contact her for days?

She called Sophie back.

"I hope you're not backing out on your date with Phil," Sophie said.

"Not a chance. I didn't want to get carried away with the crab cakes and forget I have something to ask you." She told Sophie about Sunday's bike picnic with Angie. "Angie has nothing she could wear bike riding. My stuff's not the right size for her but she's a ten like you. Could she borrow something of yours?"

"Sure. I'll bring some pants over when we pick you up Saturday night," Sophie said. "A bike picnic sounds like fun. Say, I'm off this Sunday and Ralph's on duty. I'd like to go with you. I'd like to get to know Angie."

"Great. We'll start out from my place around noon Sunday."

"Give me Angie's phone number. I'll call her. We can tell each other what we look like and arrange to meet at the ferry."

"And come to my place together. Good idea."

"How about food? Shall I bring something?"

"No. We'll make sandwiches here. I'll get what we need at the deli. We can pick up sodas from a park vendor."

Life was suddenly brighter, Liz thought as she hung up the phone. Dinner at the Rainbow Room on Saturday night with Sophie and Ralph and Philadelphia Phil and a bike picnic with her best friend and her new friend on Sunday.

Who needs you, Detective Pickle-Puss?

IN THE RESTAURANT, Sophie finished off the last of her crab cakes and gave a contented sigh. "I'm glad we came here. It's expensive, but we deserve to indulge ourselves once in a while."

Liz nodded. "Besides, it will get us in training for the Rainbow Room."

Sophie laughed. "I know you've been there with Wade, but this will be my first time. Is the food wonderful?"

"Oh, yes—and if you think this place is pricey, wait till you get a look at the Rainbow Room menu."

"Good thing Phil said the evening's on him," Sophie said.

Liz finished her own meal. "I'm not having any dessert. I'm stuffed."

"Me too. Anyway, if I ordered dessert I wouldn't have any money left over for the movie," Sophie said. She signalled the waiter for their checks.

Just as they were leaving the table, an argument near the entrance drew their attention. Liz caught sight of a man holding a camera and heard a woman yelling at him to back off.

"Looks like a photographer is trying to get a shot of some celebrity who isn't going along with it," Liz said as they walked to the front of the restaurant.

They got to the scene just in time to see a tall, well built woman shove the photographer against a wall, knock the camera out of his hands and send it crashing to the tile floor. A small woman, wearing a large hat, stood nearby, watching.

Liz clutched Sophie's arm. "That's Pamela and Mrs. Ritchie!"

Spewing oaths, the photographer picked up his camera and glared at Pamela. "This better not be damaged, or…"

"Or what?" Sophie asked, stepping up to him and showing her badge.

The photographer, a little weasel of a man, started to whine. "Officer, this woman deliberately attacked me…"

"Don't give me that," Sophie retorted. "I saw the whole thing. It's clearly a case of self-defense. I'd advise you to get out of here before she decides to press charges."

The restaurant manager appeared just then. While Sophie conferred with him and the cameraman, Liz turned to Mrs. Ritchie. "Are you okay, ma'am?" she asked. Calling her by name seemed unwise. Mrs. Ritchie must be fed up with being recognized wherever she went, since the Waldorf shootings.

Mrs. Ritchie's blue eyes looked up at her from beneath

the wide-brimmed hat. "Yes, thank you, I'm fine. That dreadful man. He wouldn't take no for an answer. If Pamela hadn't stopped him he would have taken our pictures and plastered them all over the newspapers. Why can't people leave us alone?"

She paused for a moment. "I'm Mrs. Jason Ritchie. Thank goodness you two policewomen saw what happened so my niece won't be blamed."

She thinks I'm a cop, too, Liz said to herself. It wouldn't do any harm to let her go on believing it. "I'm sorry about your husband, Mrs. Ritchie," she said, "and I'm sorry the photographer was so inconsiderate."

"He must have followed us in when our limousine driver dropped us off," Mrs. Ritchie continued. "It's getting so we can't go anywhere anymore. Dear Pamela, she was hungry for crab cakes and we were told they're very good here."

Someone must have tipped off the photographer that Pamela and Mrs. Ritchie were dining in that restaurant tonight, Liz thought. Maybe they'd made a reservation at the restaurant and were foolish enough to give one of their names. Well, it didn't matter.

Mrs. Ritchie glanced at the crowd of diners who'd left their tables to find out what caused the commotion. "I think we'll change our minds about having dinner out tonight," she said. "We'll just go back to the apartment. I hope no one follows us when we leave."

"We'll see that no one does, ma'am," Liz said.

A smile lighted Mrs. Ritchie's face, reminding Liz, for a moment, of the face in the high school yearbook.

"Well, thank you, Officer. I must say the New York police have been very kind to us."

Pamela appeared just then, asking, "Are you all right, Aunt Ellen?"

"Fine, darling, but how about you? That man didn't hurt you when you went after his camera, did he?"

"No, and it's lucky for him he didn't try to," Pamela replied, with a grin. She was an extremely attractive young woman, Liz thought. She came across as thoroughly nice.

Across the foyer, Liz saw Sophie and the restaurant manager gently but firmly escort the cameraman to the door.

"Everything okay now, Mrs. Ritchie?" Sophie asked, joining them a few minutes later.

"Yes, thank you," Mrs. Ritchie replied. "And thank you for helping us. You two officers have been very kind."

Sophie shot a surprised glance at Liz. There was no way Liz could let her know she hadn't actually pretended to be a cop.

The restaurant manager joined them. He was a large, dapper man, who seemed genuinely distressed that such an incident happened in his establishment.

He realized the identity of the two women the camera man had tried to photograph, and hastened to apologize. "I regret the distress this has caused you and your niece, Mrs. Ritchie," he said. "There will be no charge for your meals tonight."

Mrs. Ritchie glanced at the curious onlookers.

"Thank you, but we wouldn't be comfortable dining here this evening," she said.

"Another time," Pamela added.

"Anytime you care to come in, your dinners will be complimentary," the manager said.

Pamela took a phone out of her purse. "I'm calling the limo. We'll go back to the apartment. The cook will be gone to her room by now, but I'll make dinner for us."

"You ladies stay inside, and we'll go out and watch for the limo," Sophie said. "We'll let you know when it's here."

"I'm going to write a letter to the New York Police Commissioner and the Mayor, telling them they have a wonderful police force," Mrs. Ritchie said. "Remind me to do that when we get back to Washington, Pamela dear."

"Will you be going back to Washington soon?" Liz asked.

"Tomorrow," Mrs. Ritchie replied.

"We'd planned to go back today, but a police detective spent so much time with us yesterday, we didn't get our packing done, so we put it off," Pamela added.

Liz wondered if Eichle knew they'd stayed over another day. Probably not. It gave her a sense of satisfaction to know something he didn't.

"The detective was a very nice young man, wasn't he, Pamela?" Mrs. Ritchie asked.

Pamela nodded. "Yes, very." She laughed. "My aunt and I often watch police shows on TV where the detectives are so rough and rude. Well, this one couldn't have been kinder or more considerate."

Liz was sure Eichle could act as rough and rude as any TV cop, but she knew from experience he had a gentle nature. The D.A. was probably getting all kinds of flak about lack of progress in this high profile case. Most likely he suspected Mrs. Ritchie was withholding important information. He was counting on Eichle's non-intimidating manner to get it out of her.

"Maybe you officers know that nice detective," Mrs. Ritchie said. "George Something, wasn't it, Pamela?"

"George Eichle," Pamela replied.

Liz gave Sophie a surreptitious elbow jab. All she needed was for Sophie to say they knew Eichle, and the next time Eichle saw Mrs. Ritchie she'd tell him two officers who knew him had come to their rescue. Even if she couldn't recall Sophie's name, her description of two young women officers—one blonde and one red-haired—would be enough for Eichle to put it together and think she'd been impersonating a cop.

As usual, Sophie was quick on the uptake. "He must be from another precinct," she said. "Well, we'll go out and watch for the limo, now." She lowered her voice almost to a whisper, adding, "Okay with you, *Officer* Rooney?"

Outside, they both started to laugh.

"If you weren't my best friend I'd have to take you in for impersonating a police officer," Sophie said.

"I didn't say I was a cop. She just assumed I was."

"But you didn't exactly put her straight, did you? Did

you think she might give you some information because she thought you were a cop?"

"That might have been in the back of my mind," Liz replied.

They laughed some more. The limo arrived. They escorted Mrs. Ritchie and Pamela out and said goodbye.

"They're nice women," Sophie said, watching the limo pull away. "Very friendly."

Liz nodded. Now that she'd met them, face-to-face, she couldn't imagine either one shooting anybody.

"Pamela's a feisty one, all right," Sophie said. "I think if I hadn't stepped in, that photographer would have wound up with a shiner."

"They both know your name. When Mrs. Ritchie writes to the Commissioner, she'll probably mention you and you'll be cited for valor," Liz teased.

"You think just because you didn't give her your name, she won't mention you, too? She'll describe you to the Commissioner and it will get back to the precinct that Officer Sophie Pulaski and an unidentified officer with red hair should be commended for upholding the NYPD standards of courtesy and assistance, even though they were off duty."

"You don't think she'll really write the Commissioner, do you?"

"Probably not. She seems rather absent-minded. She asked Pamela to remind her."

"I hope Pamela has too much on her mind to remember."

"Don't worry about it. You didn't actually say you were a cop or show a fake ID."

Liz knew she didn't have anything to worry about as far as the Commissioner was concerned. What bothered her was the possibility of Eichle finding out about the incident. If he thought she'd passed herself off as a cop, this might put the freeze on what she hoped was a budding friendship.

She told herself to stop thinking about Eichle and start concentrating on her Rainbow Room date with Philadelphia Phil.

THIRTEEN

LIZ LIKED PHIL PERILLO from the moment she opened the door of her apartment and saw him. Ralph hadn't exaggerated, describing him as good-looking. The family resemblance to Ralph was there, but Phil's hair was not as dark as Ralph's and his eyes were blue instead of brown.

"Liz, meet my cousin Phil," Ralph said. "Phil, this is Sophie's best friend, Liz Rooney."

"Thank you for agreeing to go out with us tonight, Liz," Phil said, looking directly into her eyes. "Blind dates are always chancy."

"You were taking just as big a chance," Liz replied.

"Oh, no I wasn't. Sophie showed me a picture of you. Even though it didn't do you justice, I knew I was going out with the prettiest girl it's been my pleasure to meet since I can't remember when."

"Well, thank you," Liz replied. "But may I ask where a man with a name like Perillo picked up the best Irish blarney I've heard since *I* can't remember when?"

He laughed. "Before her marriage, my mother's name was Nora Flynn. I learned the art of blarney at my Grandpa Flynn's knee."

"Your Irish grandfather taught you well," she replied, liking him even more.

She was glad she'd worn the green silk. She'd been

told it brought out the color of her eyes and comple-
mented her hair. The only reason she'd considered wearing the black pantsuit was because she thought it would
make her look more sophisticated for Ralph's slightly
older cousin. Had she known he was half Irish she'd
have decided on the green right away.

She wished she had something elegant to wear as a
wrap. A cashmere shawl in the same shade as her dress
would look so much better than her tan coat. She noticed
Sophie had on a dark blue crêpe jacket dress but no kind
of wrap.

"I know it's been unusually warm, but won't we need
coats?" she asked.

Sophie shook her head. "Phil got us a limo and driver
for the evening."

"No waiting around outside for cabs tonight, ladies,"
Phil added with a big smile.

The evening was off to a good start, Liz thought,
as they left the apartment. It looked as if it would be a
winner.

IN THE LADIES' LOUNGE of the Rainbow Room, Sophie
smoothed a stray lock of her blond hair and looked at
Liz with a quizzical smile.

"Well, what do you think of Phil? Do you like
him?"

Liz paused before touching up her lipstick. "Sure.
What's not to like?"

What, indeed. On a scale of one to ten for looks, per-
sonality, sense of humor and everything else that mattered, Phil Perillo hit the top. He had all the poise and
self-confidence of a man accustomed to doing things

with flair—like ordering a limo for the evening, dining in places such as the Rainbow Room and making the women he dated feel special. Still, he showed no trace of arrogance or conceit. Also, when they danced between courses, she found out he was a regular Fred Astaire.

"I know he likes you, too," Sophie said. "I could tell by the way he looked when he first saw you. This could be the start of something."

Liz smiled. People in love always wanted to fix up their unattached friends. "You know a man as attractive as Phil has more than one Philadelphia woman interested in him."

"I'm sure he has, but Ralph says there's nobody special in his life, and—"

"I know you're going to remind me that I haven't had anyone special in my life since Wade."

The thought of Wade made Liz realize there were similarities between him and Phil. Wade, too, was handsome, successful and sophisticated. In the beginning, she'd liked him a lot—enough to confide in him about her penchant for following homicide cases. At first he'd been amused, but it wasn't long before he started saying her interest in murders was an obsession. He also said it was unfeminine and told her she must give it up if she wanted to continue seeing him.

Sophie's voice came into her thoughts. "Well, it's true, isn't it? It's time you found someone else."

"It's not that easy. Men seem to be turned off when they find out I enjoy following sensational murder cases—and I have no intention of changing."

"Wade's the only one you broke off with because of that."

"True, but even Eichle doesn't like it. You'd think a cop would be more understanding."

"Is he still giving you a bad time? I thought you said he let you in on some angles of the Waldorf case."

"His attitude is better than it used to be, and he did fill me in on a few things about the case, but I haven't seen or heard from him for almost a week."

"Well, if Phil's going to be turned off by your gruesome hobby, the sooner he finds out about it the better," Sophie said. "Let's get back to the table."

"Are you saying I should tell him about it now?"

"Sure. Why not?"

It wasn't a bad idea, Liz thought. The way things were going, it looked as if Phil might want to see her again. Better to let him know about it as soon as possible instead of springing it on him sometime in the future. The last thing she needed was a Wade rerun.

They'd been back at the table for a few minutes when the dessert cart appeared.

Liz noticed Phil eyeing her selection—a slice of double-chocolate-fudge layer cake topped with whipped cream and slivered almonds. She knew he was wondering how she had room for it after a jumbo shrimp cocktail, a generous green salad with blue cheese dressing and croutons, and an order of Beef Wellington with all the trimmings. She'd always had a healthy appetite, and after all the hamburgers and TV dinners she'd been eating lately, this meal was a real treat.

Sophie didn't hold back, either. Even though she still lived with her parents and Liz knew Mrs. Pulaski was a great cook, that didn't keep Sophie from choosing a six-inch-high wedge of lemon chiffon pie from the pastry cart.

"It's a pleasure to have dinner with women who enjoy eating," Phil said. "Too many are on fad diets these days. And what burns me up is when they order something and hardly touch it."

"Nothing like that with these two," Ralph said with a grin. "They never even leave enough on their plates for a doggie bag."

"You're saying we're a couple of gluttons," Sophie retorted.

"Appreciating good food isn't gluttony," Phil replied. "It's one of life's pleasures." He took a forkful of his chocolate cheesecake and gave a pleased smile.

"Something tells me you're a real gourmet," Liz said.

Ralph laughed, "You got it, Liz—cousin Phil's into food in a big way."

Phil nodded. "I'll admit I'm a food freak. I check out every new restaurant in town. I subscribe to gourmet food magazines and I like to cook." He gave a semi-rueful smile.

"Kind of an offbeat hobby for a man, but I enjoy it."

Liz realized she'd never get a better opportunity to tell him about her own offbeat hobby. "Hobbies are very personal," she said. "When they're unusual, not everyone understands."

Phil cast her a long look. "I get the feeling you're speaking from experience."

"You bet she is," Sophie said. "Tell him, Liz."

Well, here goes, Liz thought. "If you think being a

food freak is an unusual hobby for a man, how about a woman being hooked on homicides? I love to follow sensational murder cases, especially when I can go to the scene of the crime."

"That sounds like an absorbing hobby. Why are you looking at me as if you expect me to be shocked?"

"Don't you even disapprove?"

"Not at all. Tell me more about it, especially how you can go to crime scenes."

She told him about Pop and about Dan. She was going to mention Eichle, but decided not to. She'd only find herself complaining that Eichle fed her bits of information and then clammed up on something she really wanted to know about. Like the murder weapon in the Waldorf case, for example.

"Between my father and my boss, I feel as if I'm right up there in the front lines. I might have lost interest a long time ago if I had to rely on newspapers and TV."

"It must be quite an experience, going to a murder scene. Most women would feel squeamish."

"I never feel squeamish. I've been told this makes me unfeminine."

He laughed. "*You,* unfeminine?"

She liked the way he looked at her when he said that.

Sophie finished her dessert and gave a contented sigh. "This has been a wonderful evening."

"The evening's still young," Phil said. "Let's order a liqueur and have one more dance, and after that there's a little place we can go and hear some really good jazz. How about it?"

THEY'D JUST STEPPED OFF the elevator into the lobby, when Liz saw Juan Vega walking past with two women and another man.

She clutched Sophie's arm. "Look, there's Angie's friend, Juan. He's the one wearing the gray suit."

"The guy who followed you that night?" Sophie stared at the passing group. "You didn't tell me he was so good-looking."

Juan did look nice, Liz thought, watching him walk away. He was wearing a coat and tie. The other man was well dressed, too. From what she saw, before the group turned a corner and disappeared from view, the women had on black or navy blue pantsuits. Everyone looked fairly young.

"Do you think he's out on the town with one of those women?" Sophie asked.

"I hope not," Liz replied. Neither of the women had looked Hispanic. Was Juan two-timing Angie with an Anglo? No, there must be another explanation, she decided.

Her curiosity didn't last long. What woman in her right mind could dwell on something like this while being driven to a jazz club in a limo with the most attractive man she'd ever met?

It was after midnight when the limousine drew up in front of her building. Phil saw her to her apartment door and said he'd like to see her again next time he came to New York.

She told him she'd had a great time and said she'd like to see him again.

He gave her a light kiss and they said good night.

While getting ready for bed, she reviewed the evening.

She continued to think about it after she was settled in for the night. Though she'd had some classy dates around Manhattan, this one topped them all, and she knew why. *Phil.* He was unlike any man she'd ever been out with—and he wanted to see her again! Was Sophie right? Could this be the start of something? The mere possibility should have made her absolutely euphoric. It didn't.

Maybe she was too drowsy. Maybe she'd wake up tomorrow with the wonderful sense of excitement she should be feeling now. She plumped up her pillow and closed her eyes, letting the pleasant pre-sleep languor surround her, when suddenly, a thought stole into her mind, and as she drifted into sleep, it became a fleeting dream.

She was having pizza and beer with Eichle again, and he was calling her "Liz."

FOURTEEN

LIZ WAKENED THE NEXT morning thinking about today's bike picnic. Early-morning sunlight, streaming through her windows, told her it was a perfect day for it. Still drowsy, she looked at her clock. She'd slept later than usual. Then she remembered last night. Smiling, she settled back on her pillows and savored it all again.

She showered and dressed in blue bike pants and a white tee before she recalled last night's fleeting dream. Why had beer and pizza with Eichle overshadowed champagne and Beef Wellington and Phil? Had she become obsessed with wanting Eichle to stop calling her Rooney?

She'd just finished making sandwiches for the picnic, when Sophie and Angie arrived. It was obvious the two of them had taken a liking to each other on the way in from Staten Island. Good, she thought. She wanted her oldest friend and her newest to be friends, too.

Angie changed into the borrowed bike pants while Sophie and Liz packed the bike bags.

"Angie doesn't have a bag, but we don't need more than two, anyway," Sophie said. "There's plenty of room for my phone and my gun."

Liz looked at her, startled. "Your gun?"

"Sure," Sophie replied. "You're a cop's daughter.

You should know off duty officers keep their guns with them."

"I forgot for a minute that you're not still sitting at that desk," Liz said. "Did you have your gun with you last night?"

"No, I couldn't squeeze it into my little purse, but Ralph was packing his, so I figured that was enough."

At that moment Angie appeared, all smiles, wearing Sophie's blue-and-white-checked pants. "They fit perfectly," she announced. "Thank you for lending them to me, Sophie, and thank you, Liz, for planning this picnic."

"We're going to have a fun day," Liz said. "Are we all set now?"

"All systems go," Sophie replied.

Walking towards the subway, they saw a cruising taxi. "What do you say we take a cab to the park?" Liz asked.

Sophie and Angie agreed. Sophie hailed the cab and turned to Liz with a teasing grin. "Looks like you haven't gotten over last night yet. I'm surprised you didn't suggest getting a limo."

"Like you didn't enjoy riding around town like we were a couple of Park Avenue heiresses," Liz retorted.

In the cab, while they filled Angie in about the limo and the rest of their gala evening, Liz again recalled seeing Juan at Rockefeller Center. She decided not to mention this to Angie. Instead, she asked Angie if she'd seen Juan recently.

Angie looked troubled. "I have not seen him since you and I were in the coffeehouse. He has telephoned me many times wanting to get together but I have always made some excuse not to see him. Now he has stopped telephoning me. I know he thinks I suspect him of having something to do with the murders. He is probably hurt and angry with me."

"But now you've changed your mind about that," Liz said. "You should phone him and set things straight." As she spoke, she shot Sophie a warning glance, hoping Sophie would not tell Angie they'd seen Juan with a group of men and women last night in Rockefeller Center. Angie might think he'd been partying. This could upset her.

Sophie picked up on the vibes. "Yes, call him, Angie," she advised.

"I have already telephoned him. There was no answer. I left my name on his message machine, but he did not call me back."

"If you really go for this guy, then you should keep on calling till you get through to him," Sophie said.

"If I go for him…this means am I in love with him?"

"Something like that."

"I have grown to like Juan very much. I think of him all the time. Perhaps I am in love with him. Do you think I might be?"

"Don't ask me, ask Sophie," Liz said with a laugh. "She's more of an authority on that than I am."

Angie looked at Sophie with a smile. "I know. She told me all about Ralph. But surely you have been in love, Liz."

"Not really. Only a few infatuations."

"Was one of them that policeman who was so kind to me?"

"Eichle? Oh, no. He's not exactly infatuation material."

"He's kind of a grouch," Sophie added. "Liz and I call him names like Detective Sour-Puss or Pickle-Puss."

"I did not think he was grouchy or sour," Angie said. "He was very pleasant to me."

"Well, he's not as bad as he used to be," Liz admitted.

Come to think of it, she couldn't recall the last time Eichle had been really grouchy. But when Dan came back from vacation she'd start running into Eichle at murder scenes, and it would be *"What are you doing here, Rooney?"* all over again.

IN THE PARK, they rented their bikes and started to pedal along a tree-bordered path. The mild weather of the past few days had brought out leaves and buds, and the wintry-brown grass showed tinges of green.

"It is almost like summer," Angie said. "And what a beautiful place. It is like we are not in the city anymore."

"I'd almost forgotten how beautiful Central Park is," Liz replied. "I haven't been here since my parents brought me to the zoo when I was a kid."

"I came here to a concert a couple of years ago," Sophie said, "but I only saw the area where it was held. I guess we Staten Islanders think we have so much green space, we don't need to visit Central Park."

"Look over there," Angie said, pointing towards a row of trees bursting with pink buds. "Are those cherry blossoms?"

Liz nodded. "I think they are. I brought my camera. Let's stop and take some pictures."

They parked their bikes alongside a bench and took turns posing beneath the blossoming trees. An elderly couple, strolling by, stopped and offered to take a picture of them together.

"Three pretty young ladies, one blonde, one brunette and one auburn," the gentleman said, after he'd snapped the photo. "This will be a beautiful picture."

Liz liked hearing herself described as auburn instead of redhead. Did Phil think of her as auburn, she wondered. She knew Eichle didn't. He'd made too many references to her redheaded temper.

"Where are we going to have lunch?" Sophie asked, when they were on their way again.

"I have heard there is a lake," Angie replied. "It would be nice to have a picnic near the water."

Sophie nodded. "Good idea."

"There'll be signs telling us how to get to the lake," Liz said.

They followed the path. Suddenly, as they rounded a bend, they heard the blare of music. A moment later they saw a large group of men gathered in a nearby field. The music was coming from several large portable radios. Balloons, flags, and drink coolers set up beneath a tree indicated some sort of party was in progress.

"They're all young," Sophie said as they got closer. "Probably some boys from a Columbia University fraternity celebrating the rites of spring."

Liz observed the scene and shook her head. "I don't think so. Some of them look too old to be in college, and those flags—aren't they Puerto Rican?"

"Yes, they are," Angie said.

"This isn't the day of the annual Puerto Rican Day parade, is it?" Liz asked.

Sophie shook her head. "No, that isn't till June. This might be a Nationalist rally."

"I remember after that parade a couple of years ago, a mob of Puerto Rican men came to Central Park to celebrate, and the celebration turned ugly."

"I remember that, too," Sophie said. "They were molesting any woman who happened to be passing by, and some women almost had their clothes torn off. I wish I'd been a cop back then. I'd have herded them all off to jail."

The imagery of five-foot-five, one-hundred-twenty-pound Sophie rounding up a crowd of drunken Puerto Rican men made Liz smile. "You might have found yourself out of uniform," she teased.

"Very funny, but if one of them had lain a hand on me I'd have drawn my gun."

"If this is a Nationalist rally, maybe Juan is here," Angie said.

They'd reached the area where the men were partying, and just as Angie spoke, part of the crowd spilled out onto the path, blocking their way.

"We'd better get off our bikes and walk around them," Sophie said.

"Maybe we should turn around and ride in the other direction," Liz suggested.

Angie had been scanning the crowd, looking for Juan. "I think Liz is right. I do not like the way some of those men are behaving. I think they have been drinking."

"I didn't think alcoholic beverages were allowed in the park," Liz said.

"Only with a permit," Sophie replied. "These guys must have a permit, or they wouldn't be swilling down those beers so openly."

"Let's turn around," Liz said.

"Oh, come on," Sophie said, getting off her bike. "They're not bombed enough to make trouble. A few remarks and whistles won't hurt us. We'll just walk our bikes around them, get back on our wheels and be on our way."

"I think it's too late for that," Liz said. Several of the men had seen them and started walking towards them—none too steadily, she noticed.

"Well, looky here, three pretty *muchachas*," one said. He had a tattoo of the Puerto Rican flag on his arm and a can of beer in his hand.

Another guy, bushy-browed, bearded, and carrying a beer, said, "Have a drink with us."

"I'll handle this," Sophie muttered. Raising her voice, she said, "Thank you, but we'd like you to step aside, please. We'd like to continue our ride."

A sallow-faced, acne-scarred man cast her a dark look. "You think you're too good to join our party, Blondie?"

Bushy Brows leered at Liz. "You got your Anglo nose in the air, *novia?*"

Scarface lunged at Angie and thrust a beer can in her face. "This one ain't Anglo. She'll have a drink, won't you, *señorita?*"

Angie shook her head and turned away. He took a

long swallow of beer, tossed the can onto the grass and grabbed hold of Angie's shoulders.

"Take your hands off her," Sophie said.

Scarface gave a sneer. "Who's gonna make me?"

"I am." She flashed her badge.

Tattoo and Bushy Brows joined Scarface in whoops of laughter.

"Ooh, we're scared of the big cop," Bushy Brows said.

Scarface started pawing at Angie. She slapped his face.

He scowled. "You want to play rough? I can play rough, too…"

Just then a shout came from the crowd. "Pedro… Manuel…quit bothering those women!" A tall man who looked something like basketball great Michael Jordan came sprinting towards them.

With a muttered curse, Scarface released Angie.

"We didn't do nothin' to them," Bushy Brows said.

"We're just having some fun," Tattoo added.

"You're acting like a gang of hoods," the Jordan look-alike said. "Get out of here, all of you."

Mumbling under their breaths, the trio slunk away.

With a sigh of relief, Angie watched them go, then smiled at her rescuer. "Thank you," she said.

He nodded. "I apologize for this. Are you all okay?"

"Yes, thanks," Sophie replied. "You got here just in time." She showed him her ID. "This didn't impress your friends at all. I thought I might have to pull my gun."

Liz knew he was surprised. A cop in pink bike pants!

"I'm glad you didn't do that, Officer," he said. "A few of the boys had too much beer, that's all."

"I assume you have a permit for the beer," Sophie said.

"Yes, Officer, right here." He produced it from his pocket. "We're holding a Puerto Rican Nationalist rally. I'm sorry it got out of hand."

"Oh," Angie said, "maybe you know my friend, Juan Vega."

"Sure, I know Juan."

"Is he here?"

"No, I haven't seen him for a while and I couldn't reach him to tell him about the rally. I think he must be out of town."

"Well, we should be on our way," Sophie said. "Thanks for calling off your friends."

"I was happy to be of assistance," the Jordan look-alike said.

They got on their bikes and started off, Sophie in the lead, Liz next and Angie bringing up the rear.

"Well, that could have been big trouble," Liz said.

"Would you really have brought out your gun, Sophie?"

"I would have if they hadn't backed off and that man hadn't appeared. I was sure that scar-faced goon was going to hit Angie."

"I shouldn't have slapped him," Angie said.

"You had every right," Sophie replied. "It was self-defense."

"Suppose that man hadn't intervened and you went for your gun—if those creeps didn't disappear fast, would you have fired it?" Liz asked.

"I might have fired a warning shot, but only if the situation got extremely serious. I'd have to file a report. The last thing I need is Internal Affairs pegging me as trigger-happy my first week on patrol."

"I wonder why Juan was not at the rally," Angie said.

"Like the man said, he's probably out of town," Sophie replied. As she spoke, she glanced over her shoulder at Liz as if to remind her they'd both seen Juan after their Rainbow Room dinner last night.

Liz didn't need reminding. The incident was in the forefront of her mind. On the surface it might seem irrelevant, but she'd mention it to Eichle anyway, next time she saw him. Whenever that might be, she thought, almost angrily.

They found the lake and set up their picnic on a grassy slope where they could enjoy the view.

"Look at all the boats," Angie said. "I did not know there would be so many people out on the lake."

"Rowing on this lake has been a big thing ever since the park was finished," Liz said. "Gram has photos of my great-grandparents boating here. It was a popular courting pastime, Gram told me."

"Looks like it still is," Sophie said, looking down at the numerous couples out on the water.

"I am glad I got to see the lake," Angie said. "When I first met Juan, he told me about this park and said he would bring me to see the lake when the weather turned warm, but now..." Her voice faltered. Her face saddened. "I miss seeing him. Before I met you, Liz, he was my only friend in New York. But I have decided something. Tomorrow I will telephone Garcia y

Morales, where he works. If he is out of town, they will let me know. If he is not, I will speak to him and tell him I want to see him."

"Atta girl, Angie," Sophie said, casting a furtive glance at Liz.

Liz couldn't bring herself to encourage Angie with anything more than a nod. She felt guilty, not telling Angie they'd seen Juan the night before, and it looked as if he had a date. But, suppose the man and the women with him were business associates?

That possibility didn't fly, she decided. The people with Juan last night appeared to be Anglos. She'd heard that Garcia y Morales was a totally Hispanic firm.

She'd done enough puzzling over Juan. To dismiss him from her mind, she asked Sophie about her wedding plans. "I know you said you're wearing your mother's gown and we're going to pick out my maid of honor dress soon, but last I heard you were still uncertain about where to have the reception."

"Oh, we've decided on the Staaten in West Brighton," Sophie replied. "It's quite a long way from the church, but all the places around New Dorp that we liked were booked up. Luckily, the Staaten had a cancellation. It's an elegant place." She smiled at Angie. "I want you to come to my wedding. The invitations won't go out for a while, but save the date, the first Saturday in October."

Angie smiled in return. "Thank you for including me, Sophie."

"Bring Juan," Sophie said. "You two should be back on track after you phone him at work. Just let me know in a couple of weeks if he can make it, so he can go into the head count."

Angie looked uncertain. "I would like to bring Juan. I hope when I reach him he will not tell me he does not want to see me anymore."

Liz suppressed a sigh. The talk had taken a turn which led straight back to Juan. She might as well give up putting him out of her mind. Too many things about him didn't add up. She still suspected he'd followed her to Radio City the night she'd had dinner with Eichle. She'd seen him after the Rainbow Room last night, when Angie hadn't been able to reach him for days, and the Michael Jordan look-alike said he couldn't reach him, either and he must be out of town.

She told herself to stop speculating. Sure, Juan had been questioned in connection with the Waldorf murders and Eichle had told her he was still under suspicion, but he was entitled to a private life. Besides, she couldn't imagine how all this had anything to do with the shootings.

But, while they enjoyed their picnic, the speculations lingered in her mind. Even after it ended and they were back in her apartment, she couldn't keep from wondering about Juan.

"What a nice day we had," Angie said, settling herself on the sofa with a soda.

"Except for those punks," Sophie replied. "I noticed a few onlookers while that man was ordering the creeps off. One guy in the crowd had a camcorder. He's probably home, playing it back right now. A pretty girl being rescued from goons in Central Park."

"And probably kicking himself for not getting Angie's name and phone number," Liz added. She hadn't noticed anyone with a camera. Her attention had been focused on Angie and the Michael Jordan look-alike.

"Well, let's see what's been happening while we were having our picnic," she said, reaching for the TV remote. She expected there'd be something on the news about Pamela Enright's presence in Manhattan the day of the murders. Eichle had told her this would be released to the media during the week, but here it was Sunday and nothing had been mentioned. Her mind churned with speculation. Surely he'd talked with Pamela and Mrs. Ritchie by this time. Had he learned something which led him to withhold this information?

The news and weather report came on. The announcer said it had been a beautiful day in New York—a day which drew many residents to Central Park. A shot of the park came on.

"Maybe someone took a picture of us having our picnic," Sophie said, jokingly.

A moment later they all gasped. Someone had taken a shot of them, all right, but not while they were eating their sandwiches near the lake. The picture showed the Michael Jordan man bawling out Tattoo, Bushy Brows and Scarface, with Angie looking distraught and Liz and Sophie comforting her.

"A potentially ugly incident was averted today when an unidentified man attending a nearby Puerto Rican Nationalist rally defended a young woman cyclist from the advances of three Puerto Rican men under the influence of alcohol," a female reporter stated. "According to bystanders, the men also accosted the young woman's two companions."

The reporter went on to say the incident ended quickly

and peaceably, but was reminiscent of the disgraceful conduct of Puerto Rican men after the annual Puerto Rican Day parade several years ago. "Had it not been for the swift action of that one man, it might have developed into the same outrageous kind of incident."

The coverage of the adventure ended. They stared at each other in stunned silence for a moment before Sophie said, "Hey, Angie, my pants looked good on you!"

They all laughed.

"Maybe they looked too good," Angie said. "Maybe we all looked too good in our bike pants."

"Well, our pants and our faces are on the news tonight, but thank goodness nobody got our names," Liz said.

Sophie nodded. "And thank goodness I didn't go for my gun. I'd never live that down—being on TV looking like Annie Oakley."

"That guy with the camcorder—I guess he works for a TV channel," Liz said.

"Or maybe he was just someone taking pictures in the park and knew this would make a good item to sell to the TV channel," Sophie replied.

"Whatever he was, it did make a good item," Angie said. "The picture was very clear. You could even see that man's tattoo."

"All of us were clearly recognizable, too," Liz said. She knew Mom and Pop wouldn't see the telecast—it was local—but she might get a phone call from Gram any minute now.

Sophie wanted to make the 6:30 ferry, so she and

Angie left soon after watching the newscast. They were barely out the door when the phone rang.

Liz picked up. "Gram?"

"No," a familiar voice said. "This isn't Grandma— it's the big, bad wolf."

"Very funny, Eichle," she said. She thought of adding, "It's about time you got in touch," but decided against it. He realized she depended on him for information. She didn't want to give him the satisfaction of knowing how great the dependency was.

She knew he had on his Detective Sour-Puss face when he said, "Well, Rooney, you did it again."

"Did what?" she retorted. But she knew exactly what he meant. He'd seen the TV footage of their encounter with the Puerto Ricans. Just because she'd been involved in a couple of incidents recently, he probably blamed her for today's confrontation.

"This wasn't my fault," she said, without waiting for him to reply. She knew she sounded defensive. He'd take that to mean she felt guilty. "Why are you always so quick to assume I deliberately look for trouble?"

"I never said you do it deliberately." His voice took on a less chiding tone. "You and Sophie looked none the worse for the experience. How's Angie?"

"Of course she was upset for a few minutes, but she got over it."

"Well, I just wanted to see if you were okay," he said.

"Is that all you have to say? Aren't you going to let me know what's been happening with the case all week?"

"Not over the phone."

"When then?" She was annoyed with herself for begging. "Oh, forget it," she said, feeling humiliated.

"I'll get back to you in a couple of days, Rooney."

She wanted to retort, "That's what you always say." Instead, she swallowed her rising aggravation, saying, "Thanks for being concerned about us, Eichle. Goodbye."

More waiting, she thought. More speculating about Mrs. Ritchie and Pamela. More puzzling over the gun.

A sudden bright thought pierced the gloom of her frustration. She'd get some answers regarding the gun very soon. Dan would be back from vacation this coming week, probably tomorrow.

FIFTEEN

WHAT A WELCOME SIGHT to see Dan in his office the following morning and notice the crude, wooden *Dr. Switzer* plaque his son had made years ago in summer camp, back on his desk.

"I thought of you while I was away, Lizzie," he said. "I know you've been into those murders at the Waldorf."

"Not as far as I wanted to," she replied.

He gave an understanding grin. "No crime scene this time."

"No, but Eichle showed me some photos taken at the scene and let me in on a few things. He's been a clam about the gun, though. I don't even know what kind it was, and I don't know how many shots were fired."

Dan shuffled some papers on his desk. "I've been going over the lab reports concerning the gun. They're incomplete. What's been puzzling you?"

"In the photos taken at the crime scene, I got the impression there'd been a struggle for the gun. The woman, especially, looked disheveled. I've been assuming it went off twice during a struggle and killed them both. Do you think that's what happened?"

"I'll finish going over these reports and get back to you later," he replied.

She gave a grateful smile. "Thanks, Dan." Now that he was on the job again, she'd get some answers.

ANGIE PHONED AT 11:30. She was on her lunch break, she said. She sounded upset.

"What's wrong?" Liz asked.

"I telephoned Garcia y Morales and asked to speak to Juan. I was told he no longer works there. Then I tried to reach him at his apartment but his phone has been disconnected and no new number was given." Her voice broke. "What does this mean, Liz? Has he gone from New York to avoid more police questioning?"

Replying was difficult. Liz didn't want to let Angie know she'd seen Juan Saturday night and was sure he hadn't left New York, but she knew Angie would question her and it would all come out that he might have been partying. It seemed obvious that Angie was in love with Juan. This would hurt her.

"It doesn't mean he's left the city," she managed to say. "He could have changed jobs and moved to another apartment."

"If that is what he did, would he not have a new telephone number?"

"Most likely the phone company hasn't given him his new number yet." She knew that was lame, but Angie needed some sort of explanation.

"The man who helped us in the park yesterday, he told me he could not reach Juan to tell him about the rally," Angie said. "I know the Puerto Rican Nationalist movement is very important to Juan. It seems strange that he would not keep in touch with others in the organization. What if he has been injured in an accident and he is in a hospital, unconscious, and nobody at the hospital knows who should be notified?"

For a moment Liz thought of letting Angie know she'd seen Juan Saturday night, but decided against it. She'd wait another day or so. If he didn't get in touch with Angie, she'd tell her. This might upset Angie, but at least she'd know he was all right.

Meanwhile, she tried to ease Angie's concern. "You're letting your imagination run away with you," she said. "Leaving his job and having his phone disconnected wouldn't mean he'd met with an accident. Please stop worrying, Angie."

"Of course you are right and I am being foolish," Angie said. "Thank you for your advice. I feel better now. You always cheer me up, Liz."

They said goodbye. Liz felt as if she could use some cheering up herself. Withholding information was no better than lying. *You'd better get in touch with Angie soon, Juan Vega.*

SOPHIE PHONED LATER in the day.

"Guess what?" she asked. Liz could tell by her voice that something good had happened.

It had. Someone from Internal Affairs had seen the park incident on TV. When he saw Sophie show her badge to the man who'd helped them, he knew she was a cop.

"Of course he didn't have any idea who I was but he called some precincts and described me and finally found out," Sophie said. She laughed. "Can you believe he phoned me today and commended me for showing restraint in a tense situation?"

"Wow. Aren't you thankful you didn't go for your gun?"

"You bet. I've learned something from this. Can you imagine if this Internal Affairs guy had tuned in and there I was flashing my badge and waving my gun?"

Liz thought of Sophie's dream of someday becoming a homicide detective. "This will look good on your record when you apply for detective training," she said.

DAN CAME TO HER DESK just before quitting time. "Okay, Lizzie," he said. "Three shots were fired—two into the woman's chest, and one into the senator's neck. It penetrated his throat. Both victims couldn't have been shot in a struggle for the gun. The trajectory of the bullet that hit the senator rules that out."

Liz recalled the crime scene photo. Nadine looked as if she'd put up a fight. "Are you saying there was no struggle?" she asked.

Dan shook his head. "There was a struggle, all right. There were powder burns on both victims' hands. But it looks like the killer got control of the gun after he shot the woman, and then shot the senator. The slug in the senator's neck was distorted, possibly due to heat from the third shot. The gun is an old, single-action revolver dating back to the 1920s or '30s. Not many of those around anymore. And an initial was scratched into the handle. Looked like a 'B.'"

The kind of gun a collector would own!

Going home on the subway, she thought about this and everything else Dan had told her. It no longer seemed a remote possibility that the murder weapon had come from Senator Ritchie's collection. If there was such a collection. Eichle wasn't sure about that yet, but Pop said if there was a collection it had to be a secret known only to the senator and his wife. Didn't that point directly at Mrs. Ritchie?

In spite of Mrs. Ritchie's air-tight alibi, she'd suspected her from the first, but now that she'd met her, the idea of this nice little lady sneaking a gun out of her husband's collection for the purpose of scaring her husband and Nadine seemed preposterous. And the notion of premeditated murder was even more so. Still, she'd followed enough homicides to know that the person who seemed the most innocent often turned out to be the guilty one.

If the killer were a small woman, she'd have been overpowered in a two-against-one struggle for the gun. That would seem to scratch Mrs. Ritchie. She'd have to be a black belt in karate to get the best of both her husband and Nadine. But, just as Mrs. Ritchie (sans karate) could not have overpowered the victims, a woman the size of Pamela Enright possibly could have. She recalled how Pamela had dealt with the photographer in the restaurant. But Pamela also seemed too nice a person to have anything to do with the shootings.

She felt as if she were going around in circles with this case.

When she got to her apartment, she had to admit she was no closer to figuring out who committed these murders than she was when news about them first broke. There were too many extraneous factors in the case. The nightgown, for example. Eichle said Mrs. Ritchie had insisted her husband purchased it for *her*. If Mrs.

Ritchie was not closing her eyes to the obvious, she was knowingly making a feeble explanation.

She made a salad, microwaved a frank and some canned beans and turned on the TV. She'd take a break by watching a movie while she ate, she decided. But she couldn't resist turning to the news channel first, just to see if anything had developed in the case.

A newscaster was in the middle of a spiel about Pamela. Police had announced that two sources had placed her in Manhattan the day of the murders, but according to police, a companion who'd been with her the entire time stated they'd been nowhere near the Waldorf.

This would seem to absolve Pamela, Liz thought. Again, she reviewed everything she'd learned about the case. She found herself back at square one and Mrs. Ritchie, the only one in the puzzle around whom the pieces fit.

Again, she imagined what could have happened. Mrs. Ritchie had found out about her husband's tryst at the Waldorf. She'd taken a gun out of his collection and hopped a plane to New York. Forget airport security and her alibi. That could be figured out later. Right now it looked like Mrs. Ritchie had gone to Manhattan to confront him and the other woman in the Waldorf. She'd only intended to scare them, but things went awry.

After the shooting, she'd panicked and run from the scene, leaving the gun behind and the door ajar. When Ms. Extra Large walked into the suite and discovered the bodies, she also fled, too horrified and fearful of implication to report it.

Only the sworn statement of Mrs. Ritchie's maid and

the doorman kept all the pieces from fitting. But she hadn't forgotten what Pop told her.

"Even an airtight alibi can develop a puncture."

Having met Mrs. Ritchie face-to-face, she found this imagined scenario hard to believe. She knew she shouldn't let personal feelings get in the way of conclusions, but the fact remained, the senator and Nadine had been shot with the kind of gun only a collector would own. If it turned out the senator still had a gun collection, even Eichle would have to admit this implicated Mrs. Ritchie.

Whether or not Mrs. Ritchie had been at the scene of the shooting—whether or not she'd had her hands on the gun—Liz's instincts told her Mrs. Ritchie knew more about the murder weapon than she was admitting. This nice little lady was involved with that antique revolver right up to her wide-brimmed hat.

SIXTEEN

EICHLE PHONED HER at work just before noon the next day. "Can you meet me for a quick bite at the deli near your office?"

"Sure—if it's not too quick for you to fill me in on a few things."

"We'll have time for that," he said.

He was waiting outside the deli when she got there. He looked as if he needed a good night's sleep. This case must be wearing him down, she thought. No doubt the murder of a United States senator here in the city had the Mayor, the Police Commissioner, the District Attorney and a host of politicians and outraged citizens in an uproar. The D.A. was probably pressuring for an arrest.

In the deli, they got coffee and pastrami sandwiches on rye, and squeezed into seats at a tiny table wedged between the cold cuts counter and a display of cheeses.

"Have you recovered from your adventure in the park?" he asked.

"I didn't think we were going to discuss that."

"Just making sure you're okay."

"Thanks for your concern. I'm fine."

His mention of the park incident made her think of the Michael Jordan look-alike, and how he said he hadn't been able to contact Juan, and then Angie finding out he'd left his job and moved out of his apartment without a trace.

"Before you tell me what you've been up to all last week, I have something to ask you," she said. "Is Juan Vega still on your suspect list?"

She noticed he looked slightly startled. "Why are you asking about Vega?"

"Because he's left his job and moved out of his apartment. If he's still a suspect, wouldn't he have to keep you informed of his whereabouts?"

"How did you know he left his job and moved?"

She told him, adding, "I can understand he might be mad at Angie, but don't you think it's strange he wouldn't let his Puerto Rican buddies know where he's gone?"

"Sounds like you think he moved out of the city to evade further questioning."

"Wrong. I know he's still in New York. I saw him in the 30 Rock building last Saturday night."

"Oh?" For a moment she thought that was all he intended to say. "Did you talk with him?" he added.

"No. He didn't see me. He was passing by with some people while we were coming out of the elevator."

Eichle picked up his sandwich and tucked a large piece of overhanging pastrami back between the bread slices. "You were in Rockefeller Center Saturday night?" he asked, taking a bite.

"Yes, we had dinner at the Rainbow Room."

He cast her a curious look. "You back with that Harvard man?"

How did he know about Wade? "No," she replied.

He smiled. "That's good. According to your father, he was an arrogant jerk."

There were very few times in her life when she'd been annoyed with Pop. This was one of them. The idea of him discussing her social life with Eichle brought her close to anger.

"Well, I hope the two of you enjoyed talking about something that's none of your business," she said.

"Whoa! Don't get your Irish up. I shouldn't have quoted your father, but he said he was concerned you'd get in too deep with the wrong man. We didn't make a habit of discussing your social life. He only mentioned this Wayne guy once or twice."

"It's *Wade,*" she said, crossly. "And how did you know I'm not seeing him anymore? When we broke up, Pop had already retired from the force and moved to Florida."

"Remember when I was in Fort Lauderdale on the Ormsby case and you were there with your parents?"

She remembered, all right. She'd run into Eichle quite by accident. He and Pop had talked for a while while she and Mom checked out a nearby gift shop. She'd believed Eichle was filling Pop in on his old colleagues at the precinct. Instead, Pop was filling Eichle in, telling him about her punctured romance.

Just thinking about this made her seethe all over again.

His mouth twitched as if he were trying to suppress a grin. "I have something to tell you about the case. I talked with Mrs. Ritchie last Wednesday, and—"

"You've been sitting on this ever since last Wednesday?"

"Like I was trying to tell you, I talked with Mrs. Ritchie and I brought up the subject of her husband's gun collection."

He'd actually run with one of her speculations! "I guess you know Dan's back," she said. "He told me the murder gun was an oldie. But of course you knew about that, too, and you can see how it ties in with a gun collection. What did Mrs. Ritchie say?"

"She was evasive. I couldn't get her to admit he had such a collection. She said she was very busy getting ready to go back to Washington the next day and didn't have time to talk about anything not directly related to solving her husband's murder. That's how we left it—but only temporarily."

"Was Pamela there? Did you talk with her?"

"Yes, privately, while Mrs. Ritchie went to do some packing. She was very forthright. When I told her she'd been seen in two different Manhattan locations the day of the murders, she readily admitted she was there. She said she told her aunt she went to Manhattan with a friend that day to do some shopping."

"Why didn't she tell her she was with a man?"

"The man she was with in New York that day is someone she's been seeing secretly."

"Why secretly? Is he married?"

"Nothing like that. He's a Washington newspaper columnist who's been harshly critical of Senator Ritchie. He's the one who thought up the name 'Senator Spotless.' The Ritchies considered him a political enemy and when they found out Pamela was seeing him they made it very clear she had to break it off or she'd be out of a job."

"I remember you told me Pamela was destitute when Mrs. Ritchie gave her a job and a home," Liz said. "I'm surprised she'd take the risk and go on seeing this guy."

"They continued to see each other on the sly. They didn't take any chances of the Ritchies finding out. They never dated in Washington."

"So they saw each other outside D.C. That's why they were in New York that day."

"Right. But there's more to it. When they were having lunch at the Plaza that day, the couple with them were her boyfriend's parents."

"Sounds like something serious."

"As serious as it gets. They drove to New York that day so he could introduce her to his parents and tell them they were planning to get married. Pamela said she intended to break it to her aunt and uncle after the senator got back to Washington."

"So Mrs. Ritchie knew Pamela was in New York the day of the murders before it came out in the news?"

"Yes. Like I said, Pamela told her she went there with a friend to do some shopping."

"When's she going to break the news that she was with the columnist and they're getting married?"

"She said she wants to wait till her aunt recovers from the shock of the senator's death. She doesn't want to upset her more."

This didn't surprise Liz. In her brief encounter with Pamela, she could tell she was an okay person. "Pamela sounds like a nice woman," she said.

"She is. That's why I held off as long as possible before letting the media know she was in New York the day of the murders. It would have served no purpose other than making headlines."

Liz decided she shouldn't be surprised that Eichle had a soft spot in his heart. Pop must have recognized this. He never warmed up to anyone who didn't.

"So Mrs. Ritchie doesn't know the man she was with is the columnist her husband detested. But she's going to know, soon, the news media will get to the parking garage attendant. They'll get the license number of the car and find out who owns it."

"They won't. The boyfriend's car was in the shop that day. He borrowed a car from a friend. Reporters will be barking up the wrong tree. By the time they find this out, Pamela will have told her aunt she was with the columnist and she intends to marry him." He paused. "Well, that's all for now, Rooney."

"Aren't you going to tell me who owns the car they borrowed?"

"No. It'll all come out soon enough."

Not soon enough for her, Liz thought. He seemed to delight in feeding her crumbs of information. She wasn't going to settle for this.

"So you let Mrs. Ritchie go back to Washington without finding out if her husband had a gun collection."

"You seem determined to incriminate Mrs. Ritchie. I told you, she has an alibi that won't budge."

"I guess I let that yearbook get to me," she replied.

He finished his sandwich, took a final gulp of coffee and checked his watch. "I should be shoving off. I'm on a case with Sid Rothman. I'm meeting him at Bellevue Hospital in a few minutes."

"Another murder case?"

"A drug-related shooting. It could turn into a homicide. Looks like one of the hoods in the hospital isn't going to make it."

Again, she noticed he looked very tired. "Were you on that case late last night?"

He nodded. "Most of the night."

Her unanswered questions hung between them, but she wouldn't hassle him anymore today. "Thanks for the lunch," she said.

"I guess you were expecting more details." He sounded almost apologetic.

She nodded. "I really thought I'd stumbled on something with that gun collection." She was still sure she had. Much as she disliked thinking that a woman as nice as Mrs. Ritchie could be involved in the murders, the circumstances could not be ignored.

"I'll get back to you soon, I promise," he said, as they left the deli.

It was the same old line. He'd get back to her soon.

Meanwhile, her mind was awhirl. *Ms. Extra Large... The murder weapon... Mrs. Ritchie... The gun collection... Juan Vega...*

But at least, this time, he'd promised.

SEVENTEEN

ANGIE PHONED LIZ at the office the next day and asked if they could meet for coffee after work.

"Sure," Liz said. Angie didn't sound downcast, but she wondered if Juan's lack of communication still worried her.

"Anything wrong?" she asked.

"Oh, no. I just wanted to see you and talk about our picnic in the park. I enjoyed it so much."

They arranged to meet in the coffeehouse near Sohms—the same place where Angie used to have coffee with Juan, the same place where Angie had introduced Juan to her, and from where he'd followed her to Radio City. Or had he really followed her? She still hadn't reached a conclusion about that. In spite of her suspicions, Juan came across as a nice guy.

Angie was already seated at a table when Liz got there. "I am so pleased you could meet me," she said, a smile lighting her pretty face. "I have been thinking about our picnic ever since Sunday. Spending the day so pleasantly got my mind off my troubles."

Liz knew Angie's troubles included the delay in bringing her mother and brother to the States. But she felt sure it also included her worry about Juan. Angie was in love with him. She just wouldn't admit it.

"I am happy I know Sophie now too," Angie said,

when they were settled with their coffee. "I feel as if I have another friend." She laughed. "I keep remembering how she stood up to those awful men. I was trembling with fear, but Sophie was not afraid of them at all. But it is good the other man came to help us before she had to threaten them with her gun."

Liz told her about Sophie's phone call from Internal Affairs.

"So those few bad minutes accomplished something for Sophie," Angie said. Her face clouded. Liz was sure she was thinking this wasn't all those minutes had accomplished. They'd led Angie to phone Juan at Garcia y Morales and find out he no longer worked there.

As if to drive the thought of Juan out of her mind, Angie changed the subject. "Do not let me forget I need to buy a birthday card this evening," she said.

"For your mother—or your brother?"

"No. It is for the little girl I used to take care of."

"The diplomat's daughter?" Liz had wondered more than once if Angie had kept in touch with the Millers, but did not want to pry.

"Yes," Angie said. "I always send her a card for her birthday. Mr. and Mrs. Miller remember my birthday, too. They always send me a gift of money."

Liz had also wondered why Mr. Miller hadn't helped Angie with her immigration problem. As a member of the State Department, surely he could have done something or at least tried.

As if Angie knew exactly what she was thinking, she answered the question. "Mr. Miller has attempted to help me get Mama and Hermano here. Because of his efforts, they are still under consideration, but that is all he was able to accomplish. I suppose I should be thankful that there is still a chance. Mr. Miller says when I become a citizen I will be allowed to bring them in." She sighed. "It will be almost four years before I can become a citizen. Hermano will be grown into a young man, and Mama—"

Liz knew she was wondering if her mother would still be alive in four years.

"Sometimes I think I should go back to Colombia," Angie said. "I could get a job in Bogota, but I do not know if I would make enough money to take care of my family." She smiled. "I do not wish to burden you with my trouble, Liz. Because of you, my life here has become as happy as it could. I am thankful we are friends."

"I'd miss you if you went back to Colombia," Liz said. "Please don't think about that anymore." She wondered if Angie was thinking about leaving the States because she'd given up hope of seeing Juan again.

They finished their coffee and decided to have dinner together in one of the nearby restaurants. By the time Liz got home, it was almost 8:00.

Rosa Moscaretti was at her window. She raised the sash and called out, "Your cop friend stopped in about an hour ago, dearie. He said he might come back later."

Eichle, taking it for granted she had nothing to do with her evenings than to wait around for him to drop by, she thought, as she climbed the stairs to her apartment. She found herself wishing he could have seen her last Saturday night with Phil. She wondered if he were at all curious about her Rainbow Room date. He hadn't seemed to be.

All he did was badmouth Wade.

Her usual routine after getting home from work was to shuck off her office clothes and get into her favorite old jeans and shirt. It had been unseasonably warm all day and tonight she felt like taking a shower too. If Eichle rang her bell while she was in the bathroom, he'd have to wait. He'd know she was home. Rosa would have told him.

She was out of the shower and putting on her jeans when the doorbell rang, followed by Eichle's voice. "Police! Open up!"

"Just a minute while I flush the cocaine," she retorted.

"You should be careful what you say to a cop," he told her when she opened the door. "If I didn't know you so well I might have taken that remark seriously."

"What makes you think you know me well?"

"Let's see—how long has it been since I was a rookie and your father brought his kid daughter into the station house one day?"

"Little did you know that in a few years I'd be a thorn in your side, showing up at crime scenes and trying to match wits with homicide cops."

He grinned as he sat down on the sofa. "It's been a while since you were a thorn in my side, Rooney. You put me onto an important clue in the Ormsby case and now it looks like you've done it again."

"The idea of the senator having a gun collection is the only clue I've given you that I can think of."

"Right. That's why I wanted to talk to you tonight.

I've been thinking things over. You deserve to know what I've found out since I talked to Mrs. Ritchie last Wednesday."

She could hardly believe what she was hearing. She sat down beside him, almost breathless with anticipation. "So, let's have it," she said, trying to sound calm.

"I didn't tell you I went to Washington last Friday and questioned Mrs. Ritchie some more about a gun collection."

"You did? Were you able to get her to admit the senator had a collection?"

"Yes. Luckily, a few minutes after I got there, Pamela left for a dental appointment. I thought it was an ideal time to put the screws on Mrs. Ritchie. But it wasn't easy. Nothing I said worked, till I told her about the murder weapon being the kind of old-style revolver a collector might like. I said I'd get a warrant to search the house and if we found a gun collection I'd let the news media know that the antigun senator owned enough firearms to equip a regiment. I promised I'd keep it quiet if she cooperated. That's when she told me her husband did have a collection of guns and they were stashed in a secret room they had installed in the basement when they bought their Washington house."

Liz restrained herself from saying, "I told you so!" "Only the senator and his wife knew about the gun room." Eichle continued. "The doors are kept locked and only they knew where the keys are."

This was even more intriguing than Liz had imagined.

"How could they keep this gun room a secret from Pamela and their house servants?"

"I was curious about that, too. Mrs. Ritchie told me Pamela's room is upstairs, on the other side of the house, nowhere near the kitchen area where the basement door is located. Pamela never saw the senator go down there. As for the servants, they were told he had a library of rare, old books in the basement."

"Did they have this same secret setup in other places where they lived?"

"Sure, especially after he ran for the Massachusetts state senate and swore he was against civilian gun ownership."

"Pop told me about that. His opponents found out about his guns, so he went on TV and lied, saying he did have a gun collection, but he'd disposed of it."

"Right. From then on he kept the collection a closely guarded secret. Mrs. Ritchie told me they brought the guns to Washington in their own van and unloaded it themselves, box by box."

"Did she take you down to the basement and show you the collection?"

"Yes. It was an amazing sight—floor-to-ceiling glass cabinets with guns—eighty-one of them, Mrs. Ritchie said, all displayed with identifying labels and listed in an inventory. The senator liked guns once owned by famous persons, she said. She showed me one that belonged to Al Capone and another that John Wayne used in one of his Westerns."

"Wow." Liz thought about this for a moment. "Did you notice an empty space anywhere in the cabinets—like there was a gun missing?"

He laughed. "Forget it, Rooney. I checked the guns against the inventory. They were all there."

"Well, okay," she said. "But Mrs. Ritchie must have known you came there thinking the murder weapon might have been part of the collection. Did she say anything about that?"

"Sure. She said something like now that I knew the gun used in the murder hadn't been stolen from the collection, she hoped this matter was closed."

"So, what did you tell her?"

"Before I could say we wanted to keep the matter open, she started talking about her husband's run for the presidential nomination. He had an extremely unrealistic viewpoint, she said. In spite of all the polls showing he didn't have a chance, he was convinced he could win and go on and be elected president. It had become an obsession, she said, and she'd grown concerned about how he'd react when it was all over and he realized he'd lost."

"She really took you into her confidence, didn't she?"

"Right. She also told me he believed the news media was against him and would humiliate him any way they could, if they ever got the chance."

"Then why did he go on collecting guns? Wasn't he afraid that would leak out?"

"He disguised himself when he went to a gun dealer. A hat, dark glasses, fake ID, Mrs. Ritchie said. And of course he paid cash and never gave his name."

"Why did she tell you all this? Was it a diversion, to get your mind off the gun?"

"Maybe. I got the feeling she wanted to tell me more, but we'd been down in the gun room quite a while and she said we'd better go upstairs before Pamela came back."

"How did you leave things?"

"I told her if she thought of anything else I might be interested in, to get in touch with me."

"You're handling her with kid gloves, aren't you?"

"Believe me, it's the best way." He got to his feet. "I have to leave."

"How about coffee before you go?" she asked.

He sat down again. "Great, but it will have to be a quick cup. I'm due over at Bellevue in a few minutes."

"The drug-related shooting?" she asked, stepping behind the kitchenette screen.

"Right. One of the junkies involved is in rough shape. We need to get a statement from him while he's still breathing."

Most Manhattan homicides were like that, she thought while she made coffee. Punks killing punks. Raw violence played out against a background of drug addiction and greed. Interested as she was in following murder cases, she could never get into that kind.

But murder was murder, whether it took place in a dark Manhattan alley or in a posh hotel suite. She had to admit she'd become a homicide snob.

Suddenly, while she brought two coffee mugs down from a shelf above the stove, she thought of Juan Vega. Eichle had been evasive when she asked him if Juan was still a suspect. She filled the mugs. Before his was empty, she'd have some answers about Juan.

"You never told me if Juan Vega is still on your suspect list," she said, handing him his coffee.

"Why are you so interested in Vega?" he asked.

"Because of Angie," she replied. She described the situation from the start, when Angie first suspected Juan was involved in the Waldorf murders.

"By the time she changed her mind about that, it was too late. Juan dropped out of her life without a trace. She thinks he might have left town to avoid further police questioning."

"Didn't you tell her you saw him the other night?"

"No, I thought she might think he was seeing another woman."

"Is she in love with him?"

"I think so. She's been terribly worried about him. I'd like to be able to tell her he's not a suspect anymore. It might make her feel better."

Eichle took a final gulp from his mug and got to his feet.

"Thanks for the coffee," he said.

For a second, she thought he was going to leave without answering her question, but on his way out the door, he said, "Vega isn't a suspect."

That should have put the matter to rest. Instead, it gave rise to more questions. Why had he been so evasive about Juan? Why hadn't he seemed surprised when she told him she'd seen Juan? And especially, when he stated that Juan wasn't a suspect, why hadn't he said "anymore"?

EIGHTEEN

SHE FELL ASLEEP that night with those questions in her mind. They were still there when she woke the next morning, along with some speculative answers.

Eichle had been evasive about Juan because he knew something about him he didn't want to tell her.

He wasn't surprised when she told him she'd seen Juan after he seemed to drop out of sight, because he knew Juan was still in Manhattan.

When he told her Juan was not a suspect, he didn't say "anymore" because Juan never was a suspect. She tried to put it all together as she made coffee and toasted a bagel.

Perhaps Juan had a police record. This would explain why Eichle clammed up whenever she asked him direct questions about Juan. He didn't want her to know Juan was an ex-con. Why? Maybe Juan wanted this kept quiet because he didn't want Angie to know. But since when did the police withhold this kind of information? She couldn't come up with an answer to that one.

Another possibility. Juan was on parole, and he'd been at a meeting with his parole officer during the time of the murders. This was as good an alibi as anyone could have. It also explained why Eichle hadn't seemed surprised when she told him she'd seen Juan, even though Angie hadn't been able to get in touch with him. He knew Juan had not left the city. Parolees were required to stay put.

All this seemed to make sense, except for one thing. Why hadn't Eichle told her Juan was not a suspect after his police interrogation? Why had he let her go on thinking Juan was still on the list?

She sighed. Juan didn't have anything to do with the Waldorf murders, but he was a mystery all by himself.

She was halfway through breakfast before she realized she'd been so occupied with Juan, she hadn't given any thought to Mrs. Ritchie and the secret gun room. Eichle had been very explicit. No link between the murder weapon and the senator's collection. Yet he'd told her she'd put him onto an important clue, and the only thing she'd told him that could be called a clue was the senator's interest in guns.

There was only one explanation. Eichle hadn't told her everything about his talk with Mrs. Ritchie in Washington.

She recalled when he left last night, he hadn't made his usual comment about getting back in touch with her soon. Just as she told herself he'd been preoccupied with that drug-related shooting, a discouraging thought struck her. Suppose he'd decided the detailed account of his talk with Mrs. Ritchie in Washington was compensation enough for the clues she'd given him? The possibility disheartened her. How was she to reach any firm conclusion about the murders if he cut her off at this stage of the game? She felt sure he hadn't let her in on everything he'd found out in Washington. Would she have to wait till it was all over the news before she knew what it was? She wished she could go down to Washington and find out for herself.

More thoughts crowded her mind, adding disappointment to discouragement. Lately, she'd felt as if she and Eichle were close to being friends. She'd become accustomed to his unexpected visits and phone calls. She had to admit she'd miss them if they ended—almost as much as she'd miss the tidbits of information he'd been giving her.

She turned on the TV. Not that she expected any exciting developments in the Waldorf murders. The case hadn't dominated the media for the past week. She wasn't surprised that today's news featured a juicy scandal involving a prominent city politician's wife and a man twenty years her junior.

"And now, an update on the Waldorf murders," the newscaster said.

The update was nothing more than a rehash of Pamela Enright's presence in Manhattan the day of the murders and the fact that she'd been with a male companion the entire time. For lack of anything new, the channel had repeated the story.

But Liz felt sure that Pamela's physical resemblance to Ms. Extra Large would not go unmentioned in the news much longer. Any day now, the *Informer* might start printing veiled references to Pamela's height and build. That's all it would take to set off a firestorm of media innuendo...

But at least the press didn't know the identity of Pamela's male companion. If he'd been driving his own car that day, it would not have been long before investigative reporters traced the license plates. It would have come out that Pamela was in New York that day with a man known to be Senator Ritchie's archenemy. It might even have been hinted that the anti-Ritchie newspaper columnist disliked the senator enough to want him dead. Mrs. Ritchie might have been shocked and angered enough to ask Pamela to leave the house.

But because of the borrowed car, none of this would happen. Sure, the media would find out who owned the car, but unless he were some kind of celebrity it would barely be worth mentioning. It certainly wouldn't make headlines.

At that moment, a newscaster advised viewers to stand by for a sensational development involving Pamela Enright, niece of the slain senator.

"Just in—the man who spent the day of the Waldorf murders in New York with Pamela Enright has now been identified."

Why was this being played up as something sensational? Liz wondered. She was unprepared for the announcement that followed.

"According to motor vehicle records, Pamela Enright's male companion in Manhattan the day of the Waldorf murders was prominent socialite Godfrey Lonsdale of Alexandria, Virginia, son of oil magnate Prescott Lonsdale and CEO of Lonsdale Petroleum. He is married to the former Helena Vanderveer and is the father of three children. Neither he nor his wife could be reached for comment."

Liz felt stunned. Of all the bum luck! Why couldn't the car have belonged to some single guy nobody ever heard of? And three children! Pamela was now branded a homewrecker, and the car's owner a straying husband. But the truth would come out. This Godfrey Lonsdale must be a very close friend of Pamela's boyfriend to lend him a car for a trip to New York, but it would take a real Damon-and-Pythias friendship to keep him from setting the record straight. As early as this afternoon, the true story would be out. Pamela's romance would no longer be secret. Too bad she'd held off telling her aunt. Hearing it via TV and newspapers would be a terrible shock for Mrs. Ritchie.

If Mrs. Ritchie were angry enough to order Pamela out of the house, probably Pamela and the anti-Ritchie newspaper columnist would get married right away. Unless the media frenzy stirred up suspicions about him. In her years of following sensational murder cases, Liz had seen more than one innocent person made a prime suspect through circumstance and innuendo.

Soon after she got to her office, Sophie phoned. She and her partner were taking a break in a doughnut shop, she said.

"I just wanted to tell you I heard on TV about Pamela's married boyfriend. I was surprised. She didn't seem the type to latch on to another woman's husband. Sorry I can't talk now, I gotta go. We'll hash it over when we get together."

Sophie would know, soon enough, what actually happened, Liz thought, hanging up.

At noon she turned on her office TV to see if the truth about the car registration had been picked up. It hadn't.

Newscasters were still harping on Godfrey Lonsdale.

She went to a nearby lunch counter for a sandwich. On the way back to the office she passed a newsstand where the *Daily News* and the *Post* were being unloaded. Headlines in both newspapers blared about Pamela's clandestine day in New York with Godfrey Lonsdale. The *Post* ran a photo of him on the front page. She bought a copy.

Back at her desk, she read the cover story details on the first inside page. It was mostly about Godfrey Lonsdale. That wasn't surprising. Very little was known about Pamela. Neither newspaper even had a photo of her. But what the press didn't know about Pamela, they made up for with Godfrey. Liz read about the flamboyant lifestyle he and his wife led, their infidelities, and their marital woes. They'd been on the verge of divorce several times, the article stated. They'd patched it up, but according to reliable sources they were again talking about a split. Wording of the article suggested that Pamela might be the reason.

Pamela was being subjected to this publicity today, but tomorrow she'd be put through worse, Liz thought. Tomorrow, the real story would be out. She imagined the worst case scenario. What if the media played up the bitter feud between Senator Ritchie and the newspaper columnist? What if this led to speculation by the public? What if the D.A. felt pressured? What if Pamela's boyfriend was arrested and indicted for the murders of Senator Ritchie and Nadine Berkman? What if Pamela was charged as an accessory to the crime?

Before she left the office that evening she checked the TV to see if the news was out about the borrowed car. It wasn't. When she got to her apartment, she again tuned in on a news program, but there still wasn't any statement from Godfrey Lonsdale about lending his car to a friend the day of the murders.

She cooked a hamburger and made a salad. She finished eating and started washing the dishes. Still nothing.

Suddenly she felt the need to talk with Eichle.

A glance at the clock suggested he might still be at the station house. If he wasn't, she'd ask to speak to one of the other detectives she knew and find out where she could reach him.

While the call went through she had second thoughts.

What if Eichle had decided he'd shown enough appreciation for her help and didn't want to be bothered? She almost chickened out. Only her need to discuss this latest development with him made her hang on.

She felt almost relieved when she was told that Eichle wasn't there, but she stuck with her idea of speaking to another detective. "Is Sid Rothman around?" she asked. Sid was a friend of Pop's. He'd known her for years. He knew all about her passion for following sensational murder cases.

Sid's voice came over the line. "Rothman here." Hearing it, she could picture his kind face. She'd never seen it without a smile. She remembered she used to think he and Eichle made the typical good cop/bad cop combo. But that was when Eichle was in his *"What are you doing here, Rooney?"* mode. It disturbed her to think he might go back to it.

"Hello?" Sid's voice sounded again. She'd let her mind wander.

"Hello. Sid, this is Liz Rooney."

His voice warmed. "Well, how are you, Miss Lizzie? What can I do for you?"

"I'm fine, Sid." After inquiring about him and his family, and responding to inquiries about her parents, she added, "I'm trying to get in touch with Eichle. I was told he's gone for the day. Do you know where I could reach him?"

"You got a problem I could help you with?" When a cop answered a question with a question, that meant he was avoiding a direct "yes" or "no." Sid knew where Eichle was.

"No problem," she replied. "I just wanted to talk to him."

"About the Waldorf case? He told me about the information you picked up. Nice going, Lizzie. Your father always said you'd make a good detective."

Would it be like lying if she gave him the impression she had some more information for Eichle?

While she asked herself that question, Sid apparently decided she *did* have another tip concerning the Waldorf case.

"Eichle's out of town," he said. "He left this morning. He'll be back later on tonight. I'll leave word for him to call you."

"Thanks, Sid." After they hung up, a sense of excitement penetrated her previous mood. Pamela's predicament was all but forgotten as thoughts of Senator Ritchie's gun collection again dominated her mind. There was only one place Eichle could have gone. *Washington*.

NINETEEN

EICHLE PHONED the next morning just as she was getting up.

"I got your message," he said. "I would have called you but I didn't get back till nearly midnight."

No need to let him know she'd lain awake, hoping he'd call. Now that he was on the line, she decided to hold off asking about his trip to Washington. First, she'd mention the matter of Godfrey Lonsdale lending his car to Pamela's columnist.

"So, what's up?" he asked.

Had Sid given him the idea she had another clue for him?

Would he have called, otherwise? "Nothing important," she replied. "I wanted to discuss this borrowed car situation with you. I'm afraid when the truth comes out, Pamela and her columnist could be in big trouble."

She wouldn't have been surprised if he said he was too busy. Instead, her surprise went the other way.

"Okay. I'll stop by your place around six-thirty tonight."

Trying to sound as if this wasn't the last thing she expected him to say, she replied, "I owe you a couple of dinners. If you have time to eat, I'll feed you." Maybe a good feed would loosen his tongue.

"Great. See you later, Rooney." She'd forgotten to ask him about his Washington trip.

Maybe that was just as well. She'd bring that subject up after they'd eaten. He'd be more inclined to talk with a good meal under his belt.

A good meal. Nothing in her fridge but some hamburger and a pair of shriveled franks. She'd have to stop at the market on her way home from work and get something. A steak, maybe. That would do a number on her finances, and payday was a week away, but if feeding Eichle a juicy sirloin resulted in loosening him up, it would be worth every penny.

Before leaving for work, she listened to the TV news.

Nothing about the borrowed car. She didn't know which situation would be worse for Pamela—having her name in headlines for carrying on a liaison with a married man known for his infidelities, or for secretly dating a newspaper columnist known to detest Senator Ritchie.

The secret relationship with the columnist would stir the media up most, she decided. When the news broke, there'd be insinuations that the columnist hated the senator enough to want him dead. That would evolve into a question. Was this hatred strong enough to make him commit murder?

What a puzzle this case had turned out to be. She was thankful there hadn't been another sensational murder. Till this one was solved, she had enough mystery to unravel.

Throughout the day she checked the news on her office TV. Nothing came on about Godfrey Lonsdale lending a car to his friend, the newspaper columnist, for a daylong trip to New York with Senator Ritchie's niece.

Quitting time came. As far as the TV-viewing and newspaper-reading public was concerned, Godfrey Lonsdale, married and father of three, and Pamela Enright, niece of the slain Senator Ritchie, continued to be a titillating item. The fact that their jaunt to New York occurred on the day of the Waldorf murders had become secondary to Godfrey Lonsdale's latest extramarital caper.

Again, she wondered if Pamela's columnist would become the subject of tabloid speculation when the truth came out. Would headlines voice suspicion that he'd murdered the senator he detested?

But hatred wouldn't be motive enough, even for the *Informer*. There'd have to be something more than that. She wouldn't put it beyond the scandal sheet to fabricate a relationship between Pamela and the senator. Pamela's statuesque proportions and the extra large nightgown would be brought into play. Raging jealousy, added to intense hatred, would provide a convincing motive.

She prayed nothing like this would happen.

On the way home she stopped at the market and picked up some things for dinner—a sirloin steak, mushrooms, fresh green beans and ingredients for a salad. She had vanilla ice cream in her freezer. She bought an apple pie.

As she left the market she noticed a liquor store nearby.

Red wine would complement a steak dinner, she decided.

She went in and bought a bottle of good Burgundy. She'd have to scrimp till payday, but that wouldn't matter if Eichle got relaxed enough to tell her all about his latest trip to Washington.

She set up the gateleg table she used when she had dinner guests, covering it with a lace cloth Mom had given her. As long as she was being that fancy, she'd use cloth napkins instead of paper, she decided, and bring out Mom's gold-rimmed china plates instead of the flowered plastic ones she used every day. She would have used the good silver Mom had given her, but she discovered they needed polishing. Anyway, her stainless steel didn't look bad on the table. Everything was ready except the steak, when he arrived shortly before six-thirty.

"Thanks for inviting me to dinner," he said. "I didn't have much of a lunch. I'm starved."

"I hope you don't have to rush off somewhere without half-eating," she said. "I have a steak ready to broil." She recalled how he'd ordered his steak the night they'd had dinner near Radio City Music Hall. "Medium rare okay?"

He nodded. "Okay. Sounds like I'm getting a five-star meal." He looked at the table. "I didn't expect you to go to any trouble."

"I eat enough hamburgers from a tray when I'm alone," she replied, stepping behind the kitchenette screen. "How about a beer?" she called.

"Good. Thanks." She put the steak under the broiler, set the timer, and filled two German mugs with Beck's.

While the steak was broiling, they'd have time for a drink and a discussion about Pamela's predicament.

"I've been waiting all day for a news flash," she said, sitting down next to him on the sofa. "Don't you think it's strange that this Godfrey Lonsdale hasn't come out with a statement? All the publicity must be embarrassing to him. You'd think he'd want to clear things up as soon as possible."

Eichle shook his head. "He and that newspaper columnist have been close friends for years. Went to the same prep school…roommates at Yale…fraternity brothers…"

Where and when could he have gotten that information except from Pamela, while he was in Washington?

"Are you saying their friendship is so tight that he's willing to take the heat for this?"

"That's part of it."

"What's the other part?"

"Lonsdale feels he has nothing to gain by explaining, and the explanation would only hurt his close friend."

Liz thought that over for a moment. "You mean since Lonsdale already has a reputation for playing around, and his wife knows all about it and doesn't care, what does he have to lose?"

"You got it."

"So, you believe he's not going to make any statement?"

"Right."

"What if someone—the wife, for example—tells reporters that he was in Washington, not New York, that day? And his kids, they'd know their father was home. And what about the newspaper columnist's parents? They had lunch with their son and Pamela that day. They know she wasn't running around town with Godfrey Lonsdale."

"Lonsdale's wife wouldn't know where he was that day. She was, and still is, on somebody's yacht, cruising the Mexican Riviera. And his kids are away in boarding schools. As for Blake's parents, he explained everything to them."

"Blake?"

"I was going to tell you—Pamela's boyfriend is Blake Galloway."

Blake Galloway! She'd read his columns and seen him on TV talk shows. He was a good-looking guy, clever and witty, who pulled no punches when it came to lambasting politicians he disagreed with. His criticism of Senator Ritchie had been especially scathing. No wonder Pamela didn't want her aunt and uncle to know she was still seeing him.

The oven timer sounded. She went and turned the steak. "I'm glad Pamela's going to be spared another round of sensational headlines," she said, coming back. "She's such a nice person." Oops, she thought. Would he pick up on this? Would she have to tell him about the incident in the restaurant?

He cast her a sharp look. "Yes, she is. I'm surprised you could know that."

She knew he'd picked up on it. "There's something I should tell you," she said.

To her relief, he smiled. "Okay, where and when did you run into Pamela?"

She drew a deep breath and told him everything. "I hope you're not going to give me a bad time because I let them believe I was a cop," she said.

"Not when you're cooking a great dinner for me," he replied, "but I hope you didn't try and pump Mrs. Ritchie for information."

She shook her head. "I didn't." Not that she wouldn't have, if she'd had the chance.

"Well, no harm done," he said.

He seemed to be in a good frame of mind. After he'd eaten, he'd probably loosen up even more. The way to a man's heart… The thought surprised her. It wasn't Eichle's heart she wanted, she told herself, but what was in his mind.

She checked her watch. "The steak's almost ready. Will you uncork the wine?"

"Wine, too? You're spoiling me." He followed her behind the screen. She handed him the corkscrew, hoping he wouldn't get wise and realize she was setting him up for information.

At the table, she was surprised when he suddenly mentioned Juan Vega.

"Has Angie heard from Juan yet?" he asked.

That sounded as if he expected Juan to call Angie. She was surprised he was interested enough to ask about them.

"Not as far as I know," she replied. "I'm sure Angie would have told me."

He raised his wine goblet. "Well, here's to the solution of the Waldorf case."

He took a generous quaff, then attacked his dinner with all the gusto of General Patton charging into battle. "You did a great job with the steak," he said. "With everything, in fact."

"Thanks." Feeling like a twenty-first-century Mata Hari, she picked up the wine bottle and replenished his glass.

She waited till he'd put away a big wedge of apple pie topped with about a pint of vanilla ice cream, before suggesting they take their coffee to the sofa where they could be more comfortable. When he settled himself with a contented sigh, she knew the moment had come.

"I know you went to Washington again," she said.

He looked at her over his coffee mug. "Yeah? How'd you know. I'm sure Sid didn't tell you."

"No, but he told me you'd gone out of town. I figured it out."

"Okay," he said. "When the news broke about Godfrey Lonsdale, I was pretty sure Pamela would set her aunt straight about this, so I phoned her and asked her to hold off telling her aunt till I could get down to Washington."

"Why did you want to get there before she told her aunt?"

"I needed to talk something over with Pamela, before she spilled the beans."

Liz sensed he wasn't going to let her know what that something was. Well, she'd keep him talking. Maybe he'd unintentionally let it slip.

"I guess you talked to Mrs. Ritchie while you were there," she said.

"Right. Pamela made sure her aunt would be out while we talked, but she came back later and of course I spent some time with her."

"Was she terribly upset about Pamela being all over the news?"

"Not really. She said it wasn't much of a scandal when all they did at the Plaza was have lunch."

Liz laughed. "Those two are like mother and daughter. When Mrs. Ritchie knows what's what, do you believe she'll actually fire Pamela and ask her to leave the house?"

"Depends on which is stronger, her affection for Pamela or her loyalty to her husband."

"I'm betting on her affection for Pamela. Any idea when she's going to tell her aunt the truth about Galloway?"

"Soon. She said she'd let me know when the bomb was dropped."

"Anything else you can tell me?"

"Mrs. Ritchie asked me to stay for lunch with them. Somehow she got on the subject of her high school years."

Somehow? Liz felt sure he'd steered her in that direction. "Did she by any chance show you her high school yearbook?"

"She did."

If he'd seen the picture of the Rifle Team, it would have been a reminder of the tip she'd provided. But was it really a tip? Though he'd seemed pleased about it, he'd made it clear that the gun found at the scene had not come from the senator's collection.

"I saw the photo of the senator with the Rifle Team," he said.

Would he have said that if it wasn't significant to the case? She started to ask him about it when the phone rang.

She reached over and picked it up.

Angie's voice came over the line. "Liz, you will never guess what has happened!" She sounded excited and happy.

"Don't make me guess—tell me." She whispered to Eichle. "It's Angie. She has good news. I'll bet Immigration is letting her family in."

"Or maybe Juan's been in touch with her," he replied.

Liz was surprised when Angie almost repeated what Eichle had said.

"Juan telephoned me!" she exclaimed.

"He did? When?"

"A few minutes ago. He is on his way to my apartment now."

"Oh, Angie..." Liz could not think of words to express her joy.

"I am so happy, Liz. I do not know how I could have thought he had anything to do with the murders."

"You were terribly upset, Angie. You weren't thinking straight."

"Well, I am thinking straight now. I want us to get back to where we were."

"Juan wants that, too, or he wouldn't have phoned you. What did he say?"

"Not much. Only that he had something important to ask me. Do you suppose that is what he meant, Liz—he wants to get back together like we were before?"

Liz had no doubts about what Juan was going to ask Angie. "I'm sure he meant something like that," she said. "Will you phone me tomorrow, first thing, and let me know?"

"Yes, I will telephone you tomorrow, Liz."

Liz hung up the phone with a smile and a sigh. "Juan phoned Angie. He's on his way to her place and it looks like he's going to ask her to marry him," she told Eichle.

"Well, well," he said.

She cast him an irate glance. "Is that all you have to say? I told you how worried she's been—wondering what happened to him, and—" Abruptly, she stopped and stared at him. "You've seen Juan, haven't you? You knew he was going to call Angie."

"Guilty," he replied with a grin.

The grin told her he knew a lot more. "You have some explaining to do," she said. She tried to sound annoyed, but she was too thrilled about Angie and Juan to be convincing.

"I know," he replied. "Do you want an explanation now, or would you rather wait till Angie phones you tomorrow?"

"I can't wait. I want to hear it all, now."

He finished his coffee. "Okay, here goes. Juan's not a Puerto Rican Nationalist. He's a second-generation American citizen and an FBI agent. When we brought him in for questioning, he had to tell us. It blew his cover. Only a few of us at the precinct know, but he couldn't take chances."

Startled as Liz was, she understood. The FBI had gotten wind of renewed activity within the Puerto Rican Nationalists. Juan had been assigned to infiltrate the organization and keep the Bureau informed.

"I can see why he had to drop out of the Nationalists," she said, "but was it necessary for him to quit his job and move out of his apartment?"

"Garcia y Morales, the firm he worked for, has strong links to the Nationalist movement. He quit his job and moved to break away from Nationalist contacts. The Bureau told him to lie low till he got an assignment in another city. He didn't have to go into hiding— just stay clear of areas frequented by his Nationalist colleagues."

"Were those people I saw him with in Rockefeller Center FBI agents?"

"Right."

"And when I thought he might have followed me, that was a chance encounter?"

"Right, again."

"But I don't see why he had to make Angie think he was a radical revolutionary."

"It was part of his cover to establish himself as a Nationalist to as many people as possible. He told me he made Angie believe this when they first met."

"And pretending to hate Senator Ritchie, that was part of his cover, too?"

"You catch on fast, Rooney."

"So why is it okay for me to know about this now?"

"Juan's leaving the city in a few days for his new

assignment, and I know you're not going to inform the Puerto Rican Nationalists that they've had a mole in their midst for almost a year."

"Juan's leaving New York so soon?"

"Yes. And you're right. He's going to ask Angie to marry him."

Liz clapped her hands, smiling, saying, "I knew it!" A moment later she looked at him in puzzlement. "How come he told you all this? Did the two of you get to be friends after his questioning?"

"Yes. We got along so well during his questioning, we kept in touch and struck up a friendship. Juan's a great guy."

"So he told you he and Angie were in love, but suddenly she wouldn't have anything to do with him?"

Eichle nodded. "He said he was sure he knew the reason for the sudden freeze—she suspected him of having something to do with the Waldorf murders. He said she wouldn't even talk to him on the phone. He was one unhappy guy."

He could have written her a letter and explained everything, Liz thought. An instant later, she realized he couldn't let her know, then, that he was a special agent.

"And by the time she changed her mind, it was too late," she said. "He'd quit his job and moved and dropped out of her life."

How differently this could have ended, she thought. Angie and Juan had come close to never seeing one another again.

She looked at Eichle. "When I told you she'd changed her mind, you passed that along to Juan, didn't you? You told him she was upset and worried when she couldn't contact him."

"I might even have thrown in 'heartbroken.'"

She flashed him a big smile. "You're okay, Eichle."

"I'm a sucker for happy endings."

"This *will* be a happy ending, won't it? I mean, there's no chance the FBI will object to one of their agents marrying a Colombian immigrant?"

"Juan wouldn't be proposing marriage tonight if he hadn't checked that out."

"Will they have time to get married before he has to report to his new assignment?"

"If Angie says 'yes,' he wants to drive to Philadelphia where his folks live, get married there, then go on to Miami—that's his new assignment."

Liz couldn't imagine Angie not saying "yes." "I wish they were getting married here before they go," she said. "I'd love to be at the wedding."

"So would I, but the sooner Juan leaves New York, the better."

Liz had been so caught up in this happy development, she'd temporarily forgotten the evening's mission—get Eichle's tongue loosened. Now she came down from her pink cloud and told herself to get back with the plan.

"We were talking about the Ritchies' yearbook when Angie phoned," she said. "You told me you saw the photo of the senator with the Rifle Team. Do you have any new thoughts about that and about him being crazy about guns?"

The phone rang again.

"Hold that thought," she said, as she picked up.

"Is this my favorite colleen?" a man's voice asked.

Phil Perillo.

"How many colleens do you have?" she asked. It was so easy to banter with Phil, and so much fun.

"Only one genuine article," he replied. "How are you, Liz?"

"Doing great. How about you?"

"Good, but I'll be even better when I see you again. I'm going to be in New York a week from today. Are you free for dinner?"

"I'll have to consult my engagement book," she said, with a laugh.

"Is that an okay?" Suddenly she became aware of Eichle taking it all in and looking curious.

"Yes," she said.

"Great, I'll give you a call during the week and give you the details."

"Fine."

"You sound different all of a sudden. Anything wrong?"

"No."

He laughed. "I get it. Someone just showed up. Okay, I'll say goodbye and leave you to my competition. Be talking to you soon, Liz."

Eichle watched her hang up. "New guy?" he asked.

She tried to sound casual. "Not really."

"Big date coming up?"

The way he was questioning her, you'd think he actually was Phil's competition, she thought. "Let's get back to the yearbook and the Rifle Team," she said.

"Sounds like you're still thinking one of the senator's guns figured in the shootings."

"Don't you think it's strange that he was shot with an antique gun and he collects antique guns?"

"I told you I checked the inventory and there was no gun missing."

"Sorry, I didn't mean to pressure you," she said. She held back a smile. By clamming up, he'd let her know he believed the senator's passion for collecting old guns was in some way connected to the Waldorf shootings.

Into her thoughts came the sound of a cell phone. Eichle dug it out of his pocket and answered. A moment later he said, "I've got to take this call."

She knew he meant he had to take it without being overheard. "Take it in the bathroom," she said, motioning towards the door next to the washing machine. At this point she was having unkind thoughts about Alexander Graham Bell.

"I thought you weren't working tonight," she said when he returned a few minutes later.

"I'm not," he replied. "I left my number with someone. I didn't expect this call till tomorrow."

She sensed he'd told her as much as he was going to, tonight. She should have known he was too sharp not to know the steak and wine were meant to achieve a kind of mental seduction. Well, the evening hadn't been a total loss. Sure, he hadn't told her as much about Washington as she wanted to know, and he'd brushed off her question about the murder gun, but he'd cleared up her puzzlement about Juan.

Thinking about Angie and Juan, she realized it was

Eichle who'd brought them together. He was an okay guy, even if he drove her batty with his dribs and drabs of information.

"Did that phone call mean you have to leave?" she asked.

He looked uncertain. "No—but maybe I should. I don't want to wear my welcome out."

She almost said, "Come off it, Eichle—you're too good a friend for that," before remembering they didn't have a real friendship. Sure, they'd made progress. He barely qualified for the Detective Pickle-Puss label anymore. But every time he called her "Rooney" she was reminded of his old hostility. She couldn't keep from wondering if some of it still lingered in the back of his mind.

If so, how could she begin to change that? Not by letting him leave when he didn't have to, she thought. But did he want to stay? Maybe he would, if she made it clear she didn't expect to talk about the Waldorf case for the rest of the evening. They'd had a great time the night they went out for beer and pizza. "Let's give the case a rest," he'd said, and they did.

"As long as you don't have to leave, there's an old Edward G. Robinson movie on TV at eight," she said. "What do you say we watch it? I'll make some more coffee."

They'd taken another step towards being friends tonight, she thought. Even though his parting words were "Good night, and thanks for the great chow, Rooney."

She was on the brink of sleep that night, when one last waking thought stole into her mind. It surprised her, because it was the first thought she'd had about the Waldorf case since Eichle said he'd like to stay for Edward G. Robinson.

That call he got tonight. She'd be willing to bet next week's paycheck that it had come from Washington.

TWENTY

LIZ WAKENED the next morning feeling too excited about Angie and Juan to give more than a passing thought to anything else.

She was brewing coffee when Angie called. "You told me to telephone you first thing in the morning," she said.

"Is this too early for a Saturday? Did I wake you up?"

"I'm too keyed up about you and Juan to sleep late. I've been waiting for your call. Tell me what happened." It wasn't easy to pretend she didn't already know.

She listened to it all again. It was just as exciting as the first time, perhaps even more so, because Angie had one bit of information Eichle didn't.

Liz could almost see Angie's radiant smile as she said, "And Juan told me something else that makes me even more happy. He says, as the wife of an American FBI agent, I will have no more trouble with the Bureau of Immigration. Mama and Hermano will be able to come to this country without any more delay."

"Angie! That's wonderful!"

"It *is* wonderful. Soon after Juan and I are settled in our new place, I will see my family again. Juan says he will find a big house with plenty of room for Mama and Hermano."

How many newly married men would be willing to include a mother-in-law and a teenaged brother-in-law in their homes? Liz wondered. Juan was a rare man.

"How soon are you leaving?"

"Juan says we should get on the road by Wednesday."

"I guess you'll tell them at Sohms, today, that you're leaving."

"Yes. I will work today and Monday and Tuesday. It is very short notice. I hope they will give me a good reference. I want to get a job when we're settled."

"Your friend Gloria in Personnel will take care of that," Liz said. "But how can you work next week? You have to pack and there'll be a million things to attend to."

"There is not much for me to pack. I rented my apartment furnished—even the dishes and cookpots. All I have to do is cancel my telephone and utilities. I still have three months on my lease, but Juan says not to worry, he will handle that with the landlord."

"I can't believe you're going. I'll miss you, Angie."

"I will miss you, too, Liz. But we will keep in touch and we will see one another as many times as possible before I leave. I would like to say goodbye to Sophie too."

"Sophie will be thrilled when I tell her about this. If you can spare an evening away from Juan, maybe the three of us could get together for a farewell dinner."

"I would like that, and I want to say goodbye to your policeman friend, too. Perhaps we could have dinner together one night? Juan told me if it had not been for him, he would have left New York without me. It is because of you and your Detective Sour-Pickles that I am now the happiest girl in the world."

Liz was still chuckling about *Detective Sour-Pickles* after they hung up.

Thinking of Eichle reminded her of the phone call he got last night. Again, she told herself it had to be from Washington. Either Pamela or Mrs. Ritchie had phoned him. Which one, and why?

While she followed her usual Saturday morning cleaning and laundry routine, she speculated about this. Had Pamela called Eichle to tell him she'd broken the news to her aunt about marrying Blake Galloway? Had Mrs. Ritchie ordered her out of the house? Or had it been Mrs. Ritchie who'd called? Eichle had probably told the D.A. he suspected Mrs. Ritchie knew more about the shooting than she'd let on.

Maybe he'd told her if she thought of anything which might be helpful, to call him any hour of the day or night. That would account for her calling him when he was off duty. But what could the information be? Something about the senator's guns? She couldn't stop thinking there had to be a link between them and the shootings.

She was taking laundry out of the dryer when Sophie phoned.

"I can't talk long, I'm on duty," she said, "but I wanted to tell you I heard the exciting news."

How in the world could Sophie have found out about Angie and Juan so soon? Liz wondered. "Isn't it great? I'm thrilled. But who told you?"

"Ralph. He phoned me last night."

"Ralph? How did he know? Who told him?"

"Who do you think told him? Phil, of course."

"Oh…" Liz realized Sophie was talking about Phil's phone call and their date next Friday night. She also realized she'd forgotten the entire incident. "We're talking about two different things," she said. She told Sophie about Angie and Juan.

"That's wonderful news," Sophie said. "I hope I can see Angie before she leaves." She paused. "So when you said you were thrilled, you didn't mean about Phil calling you."

"No. But of course I was pleased."

"Pleased!" Sophie's voice crackled with disappointment.

"Well, how about delighted or glad?"

"You mean anything except thrilled? Okay, I get it. Look, I gotta go. I'll call you tonight when I go off duty and we'll talk." She laughed. "About Angie and Juan, I mean."

Liz laughed, too, as they hung up. At the same time, she asked herself how she could have forgotten about Phil's phone call and their upcoming date. Though it was true, *thrilled* didn't exactly describe her feelings, she was looking forward to seeing him again. She scooped everything out of the dryer into her laundry basket, turned on the TV and settled herself on the sofa to fold clothes while watching the news.

No further developments in the Waldorf murders. Since nothing titillating had evolved in the supposed romance between Pamela and Godfrey Lonsdale, it was getting stale. Newsmongers had seized on another angle. As she listened to the commentary, she noticed more references to Pamela's size and even some subtle hints that the notorious nightgown would be a perfect fit.

This wasn't good, she thought. Soon, Pamela would have to tell her aunt about Blake Galloway. If Mrs. Ritchie ordered her out of the house, Blake Galloway would probably insist she marry him without delay. The worst case scenario she had pictured would materialize. Blake Galloway and Pamela Enright would be indicted by the news media even before the District Attorney took the publicity seriously.

She imagined how the case against them would be built.

Galloway, already a known political enemy of Senator Ritchie, developed a jealous hatred for him when his fiancée, Pamela Enright, told him the senator had started coming on to her. He became enraged. The day he and Pamela were in New York, Pamela wanted to do some shopping. He told her he'd meet her in a nearby cocktail lounge in an hour; instead, he went to the Waldorf to threaten Senator Ritchie with a gun. When he burst into the suite, the senator and Nadine tried to wrest the gun from him. Both were shot in the struggle. Blake fled without the gun.

Suddenly, she remembered Dan had said the gun was marked with an initial that looked like a "B." That would be as incriminating to Blake as the nightgown would be to Pamela.

She knew that this, her own idea of how it would be played out, was as full of holes as a pound of Swiss cheese, but she was sure something like it would be developed.

The only way it wouldn't happen would be if Mrs.

Ritchie didn't throw Pamela out of the house when Pamela told her she was engaged to marry Galloway. That way, the romance could be kept quiet.

Something Eichle said came back to her. *"It depends on which is the stronger, Mrs. Ritchie's affection for her niece or her loyalty to her husband."*

The phone rang. It was Angie.

"I am on my lunch break," she said. "I have something to tell you."

"Did you give your notice today?" Liz asked.

"Yes. My friend Gloria does not work Saturdays so she will not know until Monday, but I told the others in my department I am leaving to be married, and they were very happy for me. But that is not why I telephoned you. Just before I left for work this morning, Juan telephoned. He wants us to take you and your policeman friend out for lunch tomorrow. He says we will drive to a restaurant in New Jersey."

"Well, thanks, that sounds great. I'll try and contact Eichle and see if he can make it."

"We will call for you at your apartment at twelve o'clock. If Eichle is busy, we want you to come with us anyway, Liz. Eichle can come another time."

There weren't many days left for another time, Liz thought, as she hung up the phone. She'd try to get hold of Eichle at the precinct. If he wasn't there, she'd ask where he was. She smiled, remembering how she'd conned Sid Rothman into telling her Eichle was out of town. If he'd made another trip to Washington today, she'd do it again.

Eichle was at the precinct. His voice sounded brusque. "What's up, Rooney?"

"Don't worry, I'm not hounding you about the case," she said. She told him why she'd called.

His voice mellowed. "I'm off tomorrow so that'll fit in."

"Good. Angie said they'd pick me up at twelve."

"I'll be at your place before twelve," he said.

IT WAS RAINING when they drove to New Jersey for lunch at a rustic lodge in a suburban area, but as far as Juan and Angie were concerned, it could have been the sunniest day of the year. Never had Liz seen a happier couple.

"Those two can't take their eyes off each other," Liz whispered to Eichle, as the hostess led them to their table.

Eichle glanced at Juan and Angie walking ahead of them, Juan caressing Angie from shoulder to waist and back again, Angie smiling at him and gently touching his face.

"Or their hands, either," he replied, with a grin. "It does me good just to look at them. I see so much hostility and hatred."

And everything else associated with crime, Liz thought.

He needed a respite. She made up her mind she wouldn't mention the Waldorf case. She hoped Juan or Angie wouldn't bring the subject up.

They didn't.

"My folks can't wait to meet Angie," Juan said. "They couldn't believe it when I phoned and told them I'd finally found the right girl and she said 'yes,' and I was bringing her to Philadelphia to meet them and get married."

"Juan's mother got on the phone and made me feel so welcome in their family," Angie said. "She wants me to wear the lace mantilla she wore when she was a bride."

"That's great. Have you decided what kind of dress you'll wear?" Liz asked.

Juan rolled his eyes. "Here it comes—women talk!"

"You do not have to listen if you do not want to," Angie retorted, with a smile so full of love, it warmed Liz's heart. "I am going to get something at Sohms. I was thinking mushroom or eggshell silk, maybe ankle-length, with a jacket. We plan to have a morning wedding and I do not want anything too fancy or formal."

"And what are you wearing, Juan? Nothing too fancy or formal, I hope," Eichle asked, suppressing a smile.

"I've decided on a blueberry suit and an eggshell tie," Juan replied, with a perfectly straight face.

Liz noticed Eichle and Juan got along very well. Pop had told her that homicide detectives and FBI agents weren't always each other's favorite people but it would be hard for anyone not to like Juan. Through all her doubts and suspicions about him, she hadn't disliked him.

They got back to Manhattan in the late afternoon. Angie and Juan dropped Eichle and Liz at her apartment. She made coffee and he stayed for a short while before saying he had to leave.

"I told Lou Sanchez I'd stop by the precinct."

"Can't you get away from the Waldorf case, even on your day off?" she asked.

"Not with the D.A. putting the screws on us for an arrest."

"I'm glad you were able to have lunch with us, anyway."

"Me, too. I'll be in touch, Rooney."

Juan and Angie were going to leave early Wednesday morning. Liz said her final farewell to Angie on Tuesday night, when Angie's friend, Gloria Sandoval, arranged a dinner and bridal shower, after work, in the elegant Sohms restaurant on the store's top floor. Angie's friends from the lingerie department attended. Sophie too.

When it was over, and Juan arrived to pick Angie up, Liz hugged them both and wished them a wonderful life together.

She got back to her apartment, feeling a little sad. She was going to miss this new friend who'd been in her life all too briefly. They'd talked about getting together when Liz visited her parents in Florida. She hoped they would.

She'd just turned on the TV and was getting a soda out of the fridge, when she heard the news commentator mention Mrs. Ritchie. She rushed to the screen in time to see a shot of a man and a woman whisking Mrs. Ritchie through a crowd of reporters outside LaGuardia Airport. The photo coverage ended when she was hurried into a waiting car and quickly driven away.

"Acting on a tip that Mrs. Jason Ritchie, widow of the slain senator, was on her way to New York tonight, news reporters and camera crews converged on LaGuardia Airport in hopes of getting some new information in the Waldorf murder case," the commentator stated. "Mrs.

Ritchie was escorted to a car and driven off without responding to questions or making a statement. Stay tuned for further coverage."

It had been a brief, almost fleeting shot, but as Liz watched she noticed that Mrs. Ritchie was wearing her wide-brimmed hat and Pamela was not with her. She also noticed that the woman who helped get Mrs. Ritchie through the crowd and into the car was about the same age as Mrs. Ritchie. She had no idea who the woman was, but there was no mistaking the identity of the tall, sandy-haired young man with her. *Eichle.*

TWENTY-ONE

WHY HAD MRS. RITCHIE come to New York, and why had Eichle met her at the airport? The scene just played out on the TV screen in no way suggested an arrest. There could be only one explanation. Mrs. Ritchie had contacted Eichle, telling him she was ready to give him the information he needed.

The woman with Eichle had to be another police detective, maybe someone new to the squad. Unlike Eichle, there was no chance she'd be recognized. She looked to be about the same age as Mrs. Ritchie. She could pass for someone picking up a friend at the airport.

There was no point in keeping tuned to the TV news.

Whatever Mrs. Ritchie had to say to Eichle wouldn't be released till tomorrow at the earliest.

Just as she reached for the remote to turn it off, a newscaster announced that the man who'd met Mrs. Ritchie had now been identified as an NYPD detective. The woman with him was believed to be a friend Mrs. Ritchie had stayed with on previous visits to Manhattan. Mrs. Ritchie's whereabouts were presently unknown. Reporters had tried to follow the car in which she was riding, but it had a head start and they lost it.

Some reporters might have assumed the man and woman who'd met her at the airport were the friends she'd stayed with previously, Liz thought. These reporters would go to the friends' Fifth Avenue apartment where they'd be told Mrs. Ritchie was not there nor was she expected. Others might have recognized Eichle from previous encounters, and thought he'd taken Mrs. Ritchie to his apartment. This was unlikely, she decided. Eichle was too smart for that.

Also unlikely was the idea that Mrs. Ritchie had been taken to a hotel. Once reporters had checked out the friends' place and Eichle's, they'd start snooping around every hotel in the city, no matter how obscure.

There was only one place Mrs. Ritchie could have been taken—to the home of the other detective.

At this very moment, Eichle could be getting an earful of everything he wanted to know, and everything she wanted to know, Liz thought. The idea gave her an intense, restless feeling. She asked herself why of all the interests she could have pursued, she'd chosen one so frustrating.

She turned the TV off, wishing she could as easily turn off her imagination. It was too early to think of going to bed. She curled up on the sofa and thumbed through the current issue of *Time*. She picked up a book she'd started reading a few days ago and tried to lose herself in the story. With a sigh of resignation, she put it aside. She knew she couldn't concentrate on anything till she knew what information Mrs. Ritchie had brought to Eichle.

She turned the TV on again and channel surfed till she found a rerun of *NYPD Blue*. She watched this now and then. Every time she did, she wondered if Pop had talked like that when he was on duty, or if he'd acted as tough as the characters on the show. Now as she watched assorted lowlifes being foulmouthed and outmuscled by TV detectives, she wondered the same thing about Eichle.

The cop show ended. Almost two hours had passed since Eichle bundled Mrs. Ritchie into the car at La-Guardia and sped away. By now, he had all the answers. She tried to brush away the hope that he'd let her know something before it all came out in the news.

There was no point in going to bed. She'd only lie awake, reviewing everything she knew about the case and everything she wished she knew. She found an old Fred Astaire and Ginger Rogers movie on TV. It was just what she needed to divert her mind from her frustration.

Fred had just flipped Ginger over a garden hedge when the phone rang. She almost felt as if she'd been flipped over a hedge herself when she heard Eichle's voice.

"Is it too late for me to come over?"

HE SETTLED HIMSELF on the sofa. "Do I smell coffee?" he asked.

"Yes. I made some after you called." She stepped into the kitchenette and filled a mug.

"Thanks. Aren't you having any?"

"Only cops can drink coffee any time of the day or night."

He smiled. "I keep forgetting you're not a cop."

She gave a wry smile. "Yeah—right. That's why you've been letting me in on everything about the Waldorf case."

"Starting this minute, I'm going to let you in on something big. It won't be released to the media till tomorrow," he said.

Her senses tingled in anticipation. "You'd better not be kidding."

"I'm not. I've just come from a meeting with the D.A. Mrs. Ritchie flew up from Washington tonight with some information that'll curl your pretty red hair."

"Skip the sweet talk and get to the nitty-gritty."

He took a long draw on his coffee. "Listen to this and tell me if it's nitty-gritty enough for you. The gun found at the scene was the senator's."

She stared at him, stunned. "But you told me that old revolver wasn't part of his collection."

"Actually, it wasn't. Mrs. Ritchie told me he bought the gun in New York the day he was shot. Before he left Washington, he set up a meeting with a shady under-cover operator he regularly dealt with to keep his gun purchases quiet and himself anonymous. That's why we had trouble tracing the gun. The senator was very excited, she said. He was told the gun he expected to buy once belonged to Bonnie and Clyde."

Liz's mind raced. This meant a killer had not entered the senator's suite that night. The shooting involved only Nadine and the senator. He'd killed her during a struggle over her purse and the gun. She recalled that Mrs. Ritchie had told Eichle her husband was obsessed with winning the nomination and she was worried about his reaction if he lost. Whatever chance he had for the nomination, this entire Waldorf situation would blow it. Could Mrs. Ritchie's worst concerns have materialized? Had he committed suicide after he realized he'd killed

Nadine? No, she decided. The senator had stayed alive long enough to try and get his cell phone out of his brief-case and call for help. In the crime scene photo she'd noticed the briefcase, open, beside the senator's body. It had probably been on a nearby chair and was knocked to the floor when he attempted to get the phone.

"There was no assailant," she stated. "The senator accidentally shot Nadine when he went for her purse and she tried to get the gun away from him."

"And you think he turned the gun on himself after he realized he'd killed her?" Eichle asked. It was as if he were testing her for her reasoning, she thought.

"No," she replied. "If he didn't want to go on living he wouldn't have tried to phone for help. Could the gun have misfired? It was very old."

Eichle broke into a big smile. "That's exactly what happened. We figure he was in control of the gun when it went off, killing Nadine. It misfired a few seconds later. He tried to get his cell phone out of his briefcase before he died. Good thinking, Rooney. You were right on the mark."

"Thanks, but clever as you think I am, I don't under-stand how he could have been shot in the neck. He wouldn't have pointed the gun at himself unless he meant to commit suicide, and we know he didn't intend to do that."

"Right, again. You're sharp, Rooney. Your pop would be proud of you."

She wished he'd come right out and tell her how this could have happened, instead of showering her with compliments and tantalizing her with piecemeal information.

An idea flashed into her mind. "When the gun misfired, could the bullet have struck something and ricocheted?" she asked.

"It could and it did," he replied. "It hit a heavy brass lamp on the table. When we searched the crime scene we didn't notice the dent because the brass was etched with a fancy design: But after I got Mrs. Ritchie's statement, Lou and I went back to the scene and found the evidence."

Liz felt pleased with herself. Eichle was right. Pop would be proud of her. But there was a lot more they hadn't discussed.

"Will you tell me what you think happened when Nadine made her blackmail pitch?" he asked.

"The way we figure it, Nadine showed him the receipt and made her threat. He grabbed the receipt out of her hand. We found it in his pocket. But he must have realized she'd have another copy, and maybe she had it on her. She did. We found it in her purse."

Liz pictured the scene—Nadine showing the receipt to the senator and his grabbing it out of her hand, and then realizing she must have a backup copy. Perhaps she'd made some telltale move, tightening her hand on her purse, maybe…unwittingly letting the senator know the receipt was in it.

"The senator must have been sure she had the other receipt in her purse, but maybe he pretended to go along with the blackmail," she said. "Maybe he told her he had some heavy cash in his briefcase. Then he reached into the briefcase and brought out the gun."

Eichle nodded, still smiling. "He probably only intended to scare her into handing over the other receipt, but she put up a fight."

"Hold it. How come the gun was loaded?"

"We're not sure about that. If he'd been testing the gun in a bullet catcher while he was at the dealer's, he might have failed to unload it fully before he left."

"But wasn't he pretty savvy about guns?"

"Sure, but don't forget this one was very old. He might not have handled one like it before. The only other explanation would be if he'd left it to the dealer to unload it and the dealer slipped up."

"Why didn't Mrs. Ritchie tell you right away that her husband bought a gun in New York that day?"

"She didn't want it to come out that he was still collecting guns after he'd sworn on TV he was through with them. She didn't want him remembered as a liar and a hypocrite."

"What did she say about Nadine being in his suite?"

"She was hoping the police would decide Nadine was there to interview him and they were killed in an attempted robbery. When the blackmail plan came out, she insisted the *Informer* made the story up to sell more papers. She wanted to uphold her husband's spotless reputation. She didn't want the slightest hint of scandal to taint his memory."

"What made her change her mind and come clean?"

"Do you remember I told you I wanted Pamela to hold off breaking the news about Galloway till I could get down to Washington and talk to her about something?"

"Yes. You never did tell me what it was."

"Well, I told her I was sure her aunt had information

which would help solve the case, and we had to get her to come out with it. We cooked up a scheme. When Pamela got around to telling her aunt she was going to marry Galloway, she'd also remind her that if she were ordered to leave the house she'd marry Galloway right away, and it would all come out that he was the guy with her in Manhattan the day of the shooting."

"You thought after hearing all this, Mrs. Ritchie wouldn't throw her out."

"I was confident she wouldn't. Not after Pamela finished telling her everything else I instructed her to say—that the District Attorney was being pressured to make an arrest, and Galloway would be accused of the murders and she as an accessory, and that the bad blood between Blake Galloway and the senator would be a strong motive. I also told her to be sure and mention the gun was marked with a 'B.'"

"That phone call you got in my apartment Friday night—was that Pamela?"

"Right. She'd just told her aunt she was going to marry Galloway."

"Was Mrs. Ritchie angry?"

"Yes, but Pamela must have done a great job reciting what I told her to say. She said her aunt soon calmed down and assured her she wouldn't be put out of the house. She even said she'd try and forget that her husband hated Galloway, and accept him as Pamela's future husband."

Liz told herself she should have known Mrs. Ritchie was too nice a person and too fond of Pamela to fire her and kick her out of the house.

"That was last Friday," she said. "Here it is Tuesday.

Why did it take her so long to let you know she was ready to talk?"

"She wanted to think it over. She said the more she thought about it, the more she was afraid that Pamela would be implicated in the murders even if her involvement with Galloway was not made public. She told me she loved her niece dearly and could not let her go through a criminal process. She phoned me this morning and said she was ready to tell me what I wanted to know. I was tied up on another case and couldn't get away. She didn't want to wait, so she said she'd come to New York. She told Pamela what she was going to do."

"Why didn't Pamela come with her?"

"Mrs. Ritchie hoped she could slip onto a plane, unrecognized. They both thought if Pamela came with her they'd attract attention. As it turned out, someone in the Washington airport spotted her and tipped off the New York news media."

How could Mrs. Ritchie have expected to slip onto a plane, unrecognized, with that hat? Liz wondered. It had become a trademark. "So, she's spending the night with the woman detective. Are you going to talk to her some more tomorrow?"

"No, the D.A. has her full statement. She's going back to Washington tomorrow." He cast her a quizzical glance. "You saw the woman with me on TV. How'd you know she's a detective?"

"I don't know how I knew. Instinct, maybe. She certainly didn't look like a cop."

"That was the whole idea. We thought we had her looking like a Fifth Avenue socialite, but she's actually a seasoned detective who works mostly undercover." He finished his coffee.

"You want a refill?" Liz asked.

"Yes, thanks."

As she went to fill his mug, Liz felt a sense of accomplishment. Again, she'd helped solve a difficult case. But there were still some loose ends to be tied up.

"What about the nightgown?" she asked, handing him his coffee. "And don't tell me Mrs. Ritchie still insists it was bought for *her*. I know husbands can be vague about what size their wives wear, but a man would have to be pretty stupid if he thought a one-hundred-pound woman would wear an extra large. Senator Ritchie was no dummy."

"I was getting around to the nightgown," Eichle said. "In her statement, Mrs. Ritchie said again it was purchased for *her*. She said her husband always bought her a gift of lingerie when he left Washington without her. He knew the style and quality she liked, and he knew her favorite New York store was Sohms."

"How did she explain the size?"

"She said her husband knew she liked her nightgowns as loose fitting as possible because she has a neuralgic condition. Tight garments cause her discomfort and she can't sleep."

Liz shook her head. "I find this hard to believe. She's so small. A nightgown that big would fall off the first time she turned over in bed, and it would be miles too long for her. Does she really need such a large size to be comfortable?"

"She said she does," Eichle replied. "Especially around her waist. She has her seamstress alter the tops and take up the hems. I was skeptical at first too, but it's absolutely true—she has recurring attacks of what her physician diagnosed as—" He brought a notebook out of his pocket and consulted it. "Hyperesthesia," he said. "It's extreme sensitivity of the nerve endings."

Liz laughed. "Well, if she has her doctor and her seamstress to back her up, that's good enough for me, but there's something I still don't get. The senator knew Nadine had no grounds for blackmail. He knew he could prove he bought the nightgown for his wife. Why did he bring out the gun and try to get the other receipt away from her? Why didn't he just tell her to get lost, or threaten to call the police?"

"He must have believed Nadine would take the story to the *Informer* anyway, and they'd print it, and the scandal would hurt his chances of getting the nomination."

Liz nodded. "I recall you said Mrs. Ritchie told you he thought the media were out to get him. But would the *Informer* print something like that if it weren't true? Wouldn't that invite a big, fat libel suit?"

"They do it all the time and get away with it. All they'd have to do in this case was say that Senator Spotless bought a sexy nightgown in an extra large size, and his wife is barely five feet tall and weighs a scant one hundred pounds. Nothing there that isn't true."

"So, the Waldorf case is closed. Will Nadine's death be called involuntary manslaughter and the senator's an accidental, self-inflicted shooting?"

"That's fairly accurate." He was still smiling, as if he liked the idea that she'd figured everything out.

She returned the smile. "Thank you for letting me

know the case is wrapped up, before the media was informed."

"It was the least I could do. You saved us a lot of time when you put me onto the senator's yearbook, Liz."

She looked at him in surprise. "You just called me Liz."

For an instant he seemed almost as surprised as she.

"I've been thinking of you as Liz for a while now," he said.

This was a giant step towards friendship, she thought. "My friends don't just think of me as Liz, they call me that all the time," she said.

"All right. I'll start calling you that on a regular basis—Liz."

She smiled. "That sounds much better than Rooney."

He returned the smile. "I like the sound of it, too. But what about the flip side? Are you going to keep on calling me Eichle?"

She'd never thought of him as George. Now she couldn't hear herself calling him George. "I'd like to drop the Eichle," she said. "Do you have a nickname your friends call you?"

"Are you saying you don't go for George?" he asked with a frown.

The frown chilled her. She hastened to assure him she had nothing against George. "It's a fine, old name," she said. But it wasn't on the same spirit level as Liz, she thought. Was she being foolish, thinking if he insisted she call him George, that he wasn't ready for the kind of friendship she wanted?

He cast her a stern glance. "I can see this isn't going to work."

Did he mean he didn't believe they could ever get beyond Eichle and Rooney? Her heart began to sink. She ventured to look into his eyes, wishing she could tell him she'd call him anything he wanted.

A moment later the chill was gone. A teasing twinkle in his eyes told her he'd put on the frown and the stern look.

"My good friends call me Ike," he said.

* * * * *

REQUEST YOUR FREE BOOKS!

2 FREE NOVELS
PLUS 2 FREE GIFTS!

MYSTERY **W⊕RLDWIDE LIBRARY**®
™
Your Partner in Crime